CRAVING
Love & Death

❧ A Perilously Pretty Novel ❧

By

Haven Cage

ISBN: 978-0-9973811-5-3

Published by Haven Cage, LLC

United States

To my husband.

Thanks for loving me, even the darkest parts.

In loving memory of the father who loved me, no matter what.

Acknowledgments

Thanks to all my readers. Without you, my journey would be fruitless and way less exciting. I hope you continue to find new adventures in my writing.

I'm blessed to have such supportive family and friends. Thank you for kicking me in the ass when I doubt myself, and thanks for giving me strength to continue.

To my beta readers, I am always in your debt. Thank you for lending me your imaginations and critiquing skills. You help me make my work the best it can be. You ladies rock!

Dina Alexander, Tammy Becraft, Ashley Harley, Michelle Hughes, Cheryl Johnson, Heather Nelson, Elizabeth Robbins, and Diana Quiett

This is book number three, Jaclyn Lee! Thanks for sticking with me and adding your amazing golden touch (and red marks) to my writing. I would be lost without an editor, and friend, like you.

Also, a big thanks to the amazing erotic romance author, Renea Mason. Please look up her work!

GLOSSARY

Unfortunately, I'm not Russian, nor do I speak Russian. I don't know any Russians either. There are a few Russian characters in this book, so I thought I'd compile a glossary of foreign words I sprinkled in the novel for you. I searched these words and phrases on Google Translate (except for one, which I have added the link to for credit) …generic I know, but it's all I had to work with. I hope it helps.

Brat- brother

Bratstvo- the brotherhood

Brat'ya- brothers

Da- yes

Da ser- yes, sir

Demony- demons

Der'mo- shit

Devushka- girl

Ditya- kid

Hvatit- stop (what you are doing)

http://learnrussian.rt.com/speak-russian/how-say-stop-russian

Izmennik(i)- traitor(s)

Kukla- baby doll

Lapochka- sweetie pie

Poluchit' ikh otsyuda- get them out of here

Ponimayu- understand

Shlyukha- whore

Suka- bitch

Svyatyye- saints

Vladychestvo- the dominion

Vykhodit'- get off

Chapter One

I was six when I watched someone drown for the first time. 1922 was so many years ago—thirty to be exact. This…this time is different. I was a different dame then. I was just a child. My sweet innocence hid the darker impulses seeding deep in the pit of my soul. Today, the seed manifested in the twisted, thorny vine strangling me any time I took a man to bed.

Muffled gurgling sounds reached out to me, riding an escaping bubble to the soapy surface. I peered down into the blood-shot hazel eyes staring up at me from the bottom of the tub, widened in surprise— frozen in terror. My lungs heaved from exertion and excitement.

Floating clouds of bubble bath drifted over his tense face, the life there dimming by the half-second. A droplet of water dripped from the faucet and plunked against the surface, making his handsome features wave with the water. His strong hands splayed across my naked chest,

1

smashing my breasts against my ribcage as he attempted to dislodge me from atop him.

So beautiful.

His head jerked, bouncing off the bottom of the porcelain. His last efforts to evade my ill intentions resulted in failure. One of his palms lowered from my torso and pounded at the side of the tub.

They never saw it coming.

Hell, I didn't always see it coming. I'd promised myself that this wouldn't happen again, but the tall, sexy mountain of a man wouldn't leave me alone. I lied to him again and again, hoping to deter his relentless game of trying to lure me back to his pad.

"Come on, baby, let's split...go somewhere quieter to talk," he crooned with an enticing grin and confident brow. He smoothed his slick, black hair back against his temple with a comb he plucked from his t-shirt pocket. Leaning in closer, he sandwiched me between him and the wall and rested his forearm on the dark paneled wood behind me. He lowered his mouth to kiss my jaw, his warm breath heating my skin.

I closed my eyes and slid my hands up his chest, tempted by every inch of the muscles bunching under his white tee and cuffed black denim. When he pulled away, golden-green eyes scanned over my face, anxiously waiting for me to give him the answer he wanted.

He was a bad cat. That alone made me reconsider my decision to ignore men. I hadn't been with anyone in eight months, and the thought of letting this one take me home was a sweet notion to entertain. He wouldn't suspect a thing. Maybe I'd be able to leave his house with him alive. Maybe.

Dipping my chin and biting my bottom lip in feigned innocence, I gently pressed my palm against his chest in a weak attempt to push him away. "I can't. I'm working late," I whispered shyly.

His mouth curled into a wide grin. "No sweat. I'll wait," he promised, bending to inhale the scent of my hair. "You're intoxicating," he gushed, guiding his hand down the creases of my full skirt.

He'd planted himself at the bar all night, raking those keen eyes over me each time I approached the mic to sing.

Look at him. Just another victim. Another man fool enough to fall under my spell. He put up a good fight at first, but I subdued him by thrashing his head against the tiled shower wall. He never suspected a thing — until it was too late. The blow made him foggy, then I pushed him under the water. He was headed nowhere fast after that. Even now, with my fingers wrapped around his throat, his hazy amber eyes begged me to release my grip, but I couldn't. Once this side of me took over, there was no turning back. The need to reduce his life to nothing, to watch the energy extinguish from his body like a wildfire coming to an end, consumed me.

As the virile man between my thighs weakened, a surge of power flooded my body. I threw my head back and sighed, reveling in the pleasure. Tendrils of my dark curls, and the thrill of dominance, danced across my skin.

With the rush of euphoria came the crash of tragedy, though. It never failed. My buried memories were always more vibrant during a kill. And, when it was a watery death, my mind insisted on reliving the first drowning I saw, no matter how hard I'd tried to forget it over the years. It was the first domino placed in a long line of horrid moments sculpting my fate. The following dominoes ticked away, one by one, in a path of treachery and death, leading me through each miserable moment of my life.

Suddenly, the smell of salt and sea filled the small bathroom. The sensation of a cool ocean breeze swirled around me as if I were six years old again and oblivious of the life-changing event that would haunt me to this day. I straddled the man beneath me, riding his rocking body like the black waves that had steered our boat under that night sky. My vision darkened All I could see was the perilous ocean below and raging storm above.

"Tighten the rope," my father shouted over the choppy waters. Angry clouds that looked like giant puffs of smoke gathered around us. Gusts of wind caught in the massive white sails, stretching out from our boat's towering masts. I glanced over my shoulder, unwilling to let my white-knuckled grip on the railing go. "Tighten the rope, Vivie," Dad yelled again, pointing to a loosening knot tied to the sail. Rain pelted his thinning hair and ran down the deep, weathered lines of his face. He smiled, gesturing for me to secure the knot since I was closest, then lunged for the spinning boat wheel. His expression was calm and collected, assuring me that everything would be okay, but I recognized the fear in his eyes.

4

One last jerk slammed me into the side of the porcelain, then the water stilled. The room, along with my mind, quieted. I leaned back, peeling my clenched hands from his throat.

To everyone else, I appeared normal; in reality, I was a monster trapped in the lie of normalcy.

I peered down at the corpse. His black hair undulated in the blood-tinged water as I brushed my fingers along his forehead. A frenzy of emotions blasted through me: satisfaction, sadness, joy, and guilt. My fingers wandered down his stiff jaw, his neck, then along his collarbone to the large, red star tattoo decorating his right shoulder.

Narrowing my eyes, I studied it for a moment. I'd been too busy fucking him before to pay much attention. I'd seen this mark on one of my victims in the past. Jacob had one too. The style was slightly different, but still a red star. It was probably one of the tattoos they picked from the generic art wall. The two men came onto me at random times and places. Each one wore different types of clothing, had different jobs, and, from the little amount of chit-chatting we did, came from very different backgrounds.

The plague of paranoia I felt after each kill made me wonder if the men were somehow connected. *There couldn't possibly be a connection, right?*

I bent down, resting my breasts and stomach against his cooling chest. His blank eyes beamed up at me, fixed in fear.

Pushing the angst-ridden thoughts to the back of my mind, I tried to enjoy the afterglow of the first sufficient release I'd had in months. I held my breath and dipped my face into the soapy water. A building weight lifted from me once again. This poor cat...Billy, I thought, fuzzy about his name...Billy had sacrificed himself for my fleeting moment of freedom. I kissed his open mouth, then raised up, exhaling the last remnants of satisfaction I'd achieved seconds before.

Grabbing the edge of the tub, I pushed myself up and stepped out of the bath. Dripping on the red shag-rug, I stared down at the poor guy I'd rid from this world. The pangs of guilt began squeezing around my heart in full force. The high of freedom dissipated from my veins more quickly than it came.

I threw myself to the floor in front of the toilet, hugging the sides to steady myself. Vomit spewed from the sour pit of my stomach, carrying with it the shock and wretched remorse that clawed at me after each death. It spattered into the bowl only to be flushed down to some place far away. I'd learned to bury the aftereffects of my kills deep down, otherwise, I'd never be able to look at my own face in the mirror.

I hugged the toilet until my breaths evened out, then wiped the remnants of puke off my face with my forearm. I glanced over my shoulder at the smatter of blood on the white-tiled wall once more. Pushing myself up off the water-slickened floor, I fumbled out of the bathroom.

My head still swam with the dizzying effects of the rush and crash as I slid my shoulder along the wall entering Billy's bedroom. Rumpled blankets hung half-way off his bed. The river of cotton extended to the floor where they landed when he set off chasing me to the bathroom, laughing in the most charming way.

6

The toe of my cherry-red heels peeked out under the comforter, catching my eye. My brassiere hung around the bed post, and my cream silk slip lay in a puddle by his dresser. I gathered my underclothes, slowly tugging the pieces of fabric over my fleshy hips and full breasts. I clasped each hook and eye into place until my soft curves were sufficiently bound.

Approaching the standing mirror in the corner of his room, I examined the messy veil of curls framing my heart-shaped face, my cinched waist-line, and my moss-hued eyes darkened by smudged eyeliner and sorrow. The string of tiny black hearts adorning my upper left thigh drew my attention. Soon, the ink would wrap all the way around like a garter. I hadn't intended that, but with each kill, the loop grew closer to a close. As I've done in the past, I'd find a local tattoo man and have Billy's mark added, so I would be forced to remember the life I took.

I spun away from the mirror and spotted my red dress draped across the chair next to his closet. Moving toward the pile of chiffon, I paused, slipping my feet into my pumps, then grabbed the dress. I tugged it down over my head until the fitted bodice was snug around my chest and waist. After smoothing out the crinoline under my skirt, I reached around to coax the zipper up my back.

Gathering my nylons and white gloves from the nightstand, I scanned the room one last time, searching for any evidence I might have left behind. Satisfied that I had all my belongings, I left the room, and Billy's corpse behind.

It would be a long walk home.

THE MEETING

An envelope slid across the desk toward me.

"What's this?" I snarled.

"The only way to keep your family safe, my friend," he said with a heavy accent that could've only come from the mother country. He grinned, offering me a sickening view of his crooked, tartar-crusted teeth.

I glared at the man sitting across from me. Surely, he wasn't the one who ordered my attendance at this meeting. I didn't know much about the lanky crook, but I did remember my parents telling me about him when I was younger. I recalled studying those pitted cheeks, dry lips, and hooded brow in the faded photographs they showed me. They told me he was a heavy weight in the brotherhood, did the dirty work for the big boss.

"Why should I be worried about my family being safe...*friend*?" The title of comrades stuck on my tongue. These guys weren't anybody's friends.

He tsked then took a deep puff from a blunt cigar. Blowing the smoke out with his words, he said, "You, izmenniki, hid well, I give you dat." He leaned forward and rested his forearms on the desk, looking me straight in the eyes. "We found you though, ditya, and it's time to pay up." His scarred fingers flicked back the flap on the envelope and dumped out some photographs, scattering them on the dark wooden surface.

Shades of gray darkened and lightened along the contours of a voluptuous woman in a summer dress. The thin straps and fitted bodice baring her graceful shoulders and neckline did little to hide her perfect cleavage. The flower-dotted fabric flared out like a dream around her curvy hips. I couldn't tell what color her hair was, but it looked as soft as velvet.

"Who is she?" I asked, my eyes glued to the heart-shaped lips smiling back at me from the photo.

"An experiment gone wrong. Dat's all you need to know."

I glanced up at his bored expression, waiting for further explanation. He rested back into his chair and inhaled another puff from his smoldering cigar.

"What is it you want me to do?" I slouched back into my seat and crossed my arms. "You snatch me from my post, slap a hood on me, and bring me here? Why not kill me now?"

He picked at something in his teeth, holding the cigar so close to his face I thought he might singe his wispy eyebrows. Squinting through the smoke, he stared me down. "Her death means more dan yours. Besides, it's not you I want to kill." He shrugged a shoulder like we were talking about nothing more than our dinner choices being unsatisfying. "Your dear mama and papa will pay for your treachery."

I swallowed the lump in my throat, and lowered my eyes to the picture.

"She won't be easy, though," he added.

My brows pinched together, and I narrowed my eyes at him. "Nothing with you bastards ever is."

"Da," he nodded, accepting my statement as truth with a glimmer of pride in his gaze, "but she will make you work for it." He grinned. "If you survive her."

"What's that supposed to mean?" I picked up a photo from the bottom of the pile and studied it. She was sitting on the beach with her knees tucked up against her chest, toes digging into the sand from under a mass of black skirting with a poodle on it. A single strand of hair was frozen on a breeze. Her sad eyes peered off in the distant sea, like she was searching for a long-lost love out there.

"Many of our new brothers have tried to…," he cleared his throat, "eliminate her." He snuffed the tip of his smoke into an orange, glass ashtray on the corner of his desk. "We either can't locate them or found them *eliminated* themselves."

I glanced up from the picture in my fingers and chuckled. "This dame, right here, has taken out some of the most dangerous men in the world?"

He tipped his head in a half-nod then nudged his chin toward the scattered portraits. "I don't know what dey did to her, but dey broke her." A glimmer of pity shone in his eyes. "And, dey did it very young. Now, she is a weapon that backfired." His face hardened, and he looked up at me. His hand reached for a crystal glass next to him. "So, what'll it be? Your mama and papa, or her?" he asked before taking a swig of the brown liquid.

Running my thumb over the glossy paper in my hand, I weighed the glint of danger in the woman's eyes against the innocence there. Either way, I was fucked. Either way, I had to kill her. If it was the only option to save my parents, there wasn't really an option.

I stood slowly, careful not to engage the muscled meatheads behind me. Nodding, I tossed the photo on the pile of others. "When?"

"Two weeks. Keep dem." He pushed the pictures toward me, then relit his cigar. "We'll give you details before you leave." Swiping a finger in the air, he motioned for the meatheads to move. "Dey'll get you back to your post before anyone notices."

Suddenly, my head was swallowed by a black sack, and five beefy fingers grabbed my arms, tugging me out of the room.

A raspy, bellowing laugh followed me out. "Good luck, ditya, you are going to need it."

CHAPTER TWO

"Come on, Vivie!" Betty whined, plopping down beside me and wrapping her thin arm around my shoulders. "We haven't had a night out in a long time. They just wanna take us for a drink. It'll be a blast." Her bottom lip poked out, begging me to concede.

My eyes scoured the waves crashing into the Folley Beach shoreline, trying to think of a way to get out of accompanying her and the two men watching us from the busy pier. Betty squeezed me. "Vivie, you can't stay holed up in our house forever."

I'd warned her when she first made eyes at them in the restaurant that I wanted no part in her skirting around tonight. She didn't listen. Seconds later, she sauntered over to the two naval officers and sat down between them like they'd left the seat open just for her. That was all it took; they were smitten with her girlish charm and sweet, feminine wiles instantly. I wandered out of the diner and down to the beach to be alone in my misery.

Dames like Betty and me didn't settle—for different reasons, of course. She was a gal that liked to live a little on the fast side of society, refusing to conform under the usual expectations of becoming an obedient housewife. I didn't conform, but more because I couldn't make love to a man without feeling the need to murder him. I'd accepted my life of loneliness many years ago. My only saving grace from complete solitude was my catty best friend.

Betty and I met in front of the dive we work at now. She spotted me beaming up at the blend of old classic and gothic revival buildings in downtown Charleston. I was stumbling around in confusion as I searched for the location of my nanny interview. She walked right up to me and put a hand on her hip, displaying more confidence than I'd ever seen in a woman. "You lost?"

I explained my predicament. Before I knew it, she was hauling me to the back of a dilapidated barbershop where we skipped down stairs leading to a basement. She rapped out a specific knock pattern on the door. She fondly patted the man who let us in on the cheek then led me into the discrete club below.

"You'll make more money here than you ever will chasing someone's ankle-biters around," she assured over her shoulder. Betty spoke to Frankie, the owner, and I was hired on the spot.

We rented a small house in Folley Beach together and vowed to take care of each other. We wait tables, and I occasionally sing to the hordes of men and women that visit Molly's.

14

"I don't know why you insist on being such a wet rag. They won't bite," she teased with a widening grin, "unless you want them to." Her flirty gaze drifted up to the men eyeing us from the railing.

Finally, she glared back at me with an expression that said, "You are not ruining this for me," and hooked her arm around my elbow, dragging me to my feet. I fumbled behind her, struggling to dust the sand from my bottom while smoothing my skirts.

"I really don't think this is a good idea, Bet. Can't you just keep them busy yourself?" I huffed, trampling along the shoreline like a hippopotamus in heels.

"Don't be silly. They wouldn't be able to walk in the morning," she giggled. "Besides, you need to get out more."

I looked up at the two men in crisp, midnight-blue uniforms surrounded by the soft, yellow glow of the pier lights. Their mouths stretched into smiles simultaneously as they watched Betty and I climb the sun-cracked steps leading to the sea-side restaurant.

The sailors — one tall as a door-frame with soft brown eyes and blonde hair, and the other only slightly shorter with broad shoulders and olive skin that contrasted nicely next to his chocolate-hued hair — met us at the top of the steps. Betty immediately latched onto the taller gentleman, leaving me to introduce myself to the exotic-looking brunette. He lingered behind Betty and her man, seeming as bashful and unwilling as me.

I straightened my spine and held out my hand. "Vivienne." What's the harm in having a drink, right?

The seaman stepped forward. He wrapped his large, warm hand around mine, bending to kiss the back of it. His steel-blue eyes closed as his lips touched my skin, remaining there for a moment too long before he stretched up again. "Nice to meet you, Vivienne. I'm Dean."

The subtle wave of energy flowing from his palm into mine left me breathless, reminding me of the demanding compulsion I continuously worked to ignore.

I slid my hand from his, busying myself with tacking back a wayward curl that had loosened from my hair pin under the heavy coastal wind.

This poor man had no idea how dangerous I was to his health. Something about him made me crazy inside, though. I could already feel the frenzy building. That was unusual for me so soon after a kill. The sting of Billy's heart tattoo hadn't even eased from my thigh yet.

We stood next to each other, but not too close, awkwardly waiting as Betty and her new friend necked against the railing. Her lilting giggles floated into the air, charming the sailor deeper into her arms.

I cleared my throat, politely suggesting they cease their display of affection. "Um, Betty...what about that drink?"

Her sailor growled, reluctantly pulling his mouth from her neck. Betty slid her hands over her slim waist and long, tight skirt, ridding the wrinkles that had gathered with her friend's man-handling. Keeping her bright-green eyes glued to the blonde seaman, she thumbed her smeared lipstick and answered in a breathless voice, "Yes, I believe you boys promised us some booze."

The taller man stared at Betty for a moment, the yearning in his eyes clear, before pulling himself together and switching his smoldering gaze toward me. "I'm so sorry for my rudeness, ma'am. I'm Lieutenant Richard Gregson." He bowed his head, granting me a sign of respect, then clapped his hands and rubbed them together quickly. "Where do you girls suggest? This is our first time in South Carolina."

"I know a place," Betty chimed, bumping her shoulder into mine and smirking. She tucked her hand into Lt. Gregson's palm and pulled him toward the sandy parking lot. "You boys caught a ride, right? We can take my car." Richard followed behind her, glancing back over his shoulder to waggle his brows at his shipmate.

"I guess, we should go along for the ride," Dean urged, offering his hand to usher me toward the car. I smiled then tailed the two lovebirds without accepting his invitation.

Richard approached the passenger door and opened it, grinning at Betty as he waited for her to slide in. She stopped on a dime, crossing her arms over her chest and simpered. "You can't possibly be serious."

"What?" Her beau straightened, clearly confused by her rigid stance. "Are we not taking this car?" His eyes roamed over the other vehicles scattered around the parking lot then landed back on her Bali Blue Rag Top. "It's the only Hudson out here. That's what you said, right?"

Betty snickered. "Oh, it's my car, alright. That's just not my seat," she said, tugging her keys from her clutch. Betty sauntered toward Richard, slid her hand down his clean-shaven cheek, and then patted his hard chest. "You're sweet to get the door for me, though."

17

I pressed my lips together, stifling a laugh. Swaying her hips from side to side, she walked to the driver's side.

"Come on, baby," Richard groaned. "The guys'll rip on us if they see a dame driving us around!" He reluctantly dropped into the front seat and slammed the door, mumbling his frustration like a child, when he realized Betty was not giving up the keys to her precious 6-banger.

"That's no concern of mine, dearie. You're welcome to invite them to drag with me, if that'll help prove I'm a worthy driver. They'll lose their pinks, though."

Betty's daddy had taught her how to take care of cars before he died a few years before. She kept the Hornet running like a top all by herself. And she liked them fast—just like her. No one could beat her rocket, unless they had a jacked-up rod.

Dean and I glanced at each other, smirking at their silly quarrel. We opened the back doors and slid in behind our friends. Betty keyed-up the ignition. The engine roared to life, and we were wailing out of the sandy lot before we could say butterscotch.

The headlights bounced across the road, lighting our way toward Molly's. Richard leaned over, kissing and sucking on Betty's ear while she drove, inciting giggles and soft sighs from the front seat.

Wet suckling sounds layered with breathy pants filled the air. The car was full of a delicious tension. I pressed my legs together to relieve some of the heat building between my thighs. Feeling a bit awkward, I risked a side-glance at the sailor to my right.

Dean rested his shoulder against the door, draping one hand over his thigh. His other hand tugged the collar of his shirt as if it were too tight. He cleared his throat and shot a look my way.

I quickly shifted my attention out the window, praying he didn't see me watching him. A moment later, hot breath singed my neck and slick lips grazed over my skin, kissing a trail from my shoulder to my ear. I gasped, quivering from the tingling sensation radiating through my body.

"Is this okay?" Dean whispered in my ear. His hot tongue licked my earlobe.

My skin tightened, my nipples throbbed, and my breath stuttered. I exhaled a barely audible, "No." I wanted him to keep touching me, but I knew there would be no happy ending for the sailor if he did.

His long fingers skimmed over my skirt, searching for the hem, then grazed along the nylon covering my shin. "Are you sure?" he whispered, pausing his fingertips just above my knee.

With his head buried in the crook of my neck, I darted my eyes to the rear-view mirror where Betty beamed back at me. She smiled and leaned forward, turning up the rock n' roll music on the radio.

She knew what I was thinking, the arousal on my face was evident.

"Yes, I'm sure," I breathed, grabbing Dean's hand and placing it back on his own lap.

He leaned back, his eyes focusing on my mouth for a moment. With a slight nod of acceptance, Dean scooted to his side of the car.

I tugged on my bodice and swiped at my skirt, frustrated with myself.

Why couldn't I just give myself to a man and not expect his life in return?

Why couldn't I just be normal?

Why must I be a killer?

I let my eyes wander back out the window, slowing my breath to a more regular rhythm. Though my body was calming down, the hunger for Dean was consuming me like a fire.

CHAPTER THREE

The car jostled to a stop as we pulled up to the uneven curb in front of Barry's Barber Shop. Two boys dressed in tan slacks and evening jackets accompanied two young girls, maybe seventeen years old, wearing party dresses with high necklines and billowing, knee-length skirts, one powder blue and one sunflower yellow. Their white-gloved hands hooked around their dates' arms as they giggled coyly and meandered down South King Street, dodging uneven cobble stones in front of Barry's.

Barry's wasn't really a shop at all. It was a piece of history that had been passed down from son to son in Barry's family. It was a homestead that kept his ancestors warm and rooted to the South, until he later made it his place of business.

Age and salty sea air had been rough on the tri-level, leaving the wood-slat siding warped and splintered. In old southern tradition, the house was narrow but deep with tall porches on the first and second floors that stretched along the side of the house to utilize the coastal winds as a source of cooling on hot summer days. The windows on the upper floors stayed dark and the inside empty since old Barry passed away over a decade ago.

Before he bit it to cancer, Barry set his affairs and willed the home to the family who rented the extensive cellar below the Victorian Single-turned-barber shop, since he'd never fathered children. They currently kept their part of the structure teaming with movers and shakers, refusing to muck up Barry's portion. His candy cane pole and hand-painted sign still marked the street entrance, though you could barely see the red swirl or read the lettering anymore.

The surrounding business owners ran their stores under banker's hours. They closed long before the lower level of Barry's was brought to life every night, which only added to the mystery of what was now Molly's.

"Stay there, baby," Richard urged, jumping out of the car before Betty turned the ignition off. He rushed to her door and swung it open, helping her out. His eager hands pulled her against his chest where she snuggled into him and rewarded him with a chaste kiss on the lips.

I watched them, smirking, wondering if she would ever meet a guy who didn't fall head over heels for her at first sight.

The loud click of my door handle pulled my attention from their display of affection. Dean held out his hand, offering me help out of the Hornet. I hesitated, then smiled and rested my palm over his, allowing him to guide me onto the sidewalk.

Betty and Richard bolted down the sliver of space between Barry's and the next house over.

"I'm sorry," Dean said, letting our hands drop and disconnect.

Wrapping my arms around my middle, I shrugged. "Nothing to be sorry about."

The corner of his mouth pulled up in a quick half-smile. I crooked my head to the side, assessing the hard set of his lips, tight jaw, and shameful eyes. He was genuinely sorry for his advances. "I think you owe me a drink, sailor," I teased, trying to lighten the mood.

I glanced down the dark alley leading to Molly's. My best friend had disappeared around the corner and was likely already below ground, making her presence known to the bartender. She liked to keep him wrapped around her finger, toying with him for free booze.

"That I do, Ms. Vivienne. Shall we go?" Dean lifted his elbow toward me.

I hooked my arm around his, and we ventured toward the back of Barry's. "It's Vivie."

Dean looked down at me questioningly.

"You can call me Vivie."

"Okay, Vivie, what's your drink of choice?" he asked, ushering me down the narrow staircase leading below Barry's.

"I'm partial to Brandy."

We stepped into a tight dugout space in front of a dingy, whitewashed door. Dean grabbed the brass knob and turned it, leaning his shoulder into the door. It didn't budge. He backed up a pace, glaring at the door, then looked at me.

I slid past him. "Allow me," I chimed with a giggle. I knocked a beat of two raps followed by a pause and four more raps on the door. Waiting for the response, which took a minute, I became uncomfortably aware of how close Dean was to my body. His heat warmed the breezy night air, chilling my skin and sending a shiver up my spine.

He circled his arms around my waist, pressing my back into his chest, engulfing me in the sweet spice of his cologne. "Cold?"

Stunned by the delicious feeling of him wrapped around me, all I could do is nod my head and smile appreciatively.

"They gonna let us in?"

"Eventually," I answered. "There might not be anyone at the post right now." I repeated my pattern of knocks on the door and craned my neck up to look at Dean. "We'll just give 'em a minute."

His dark-blue eyes peered down at me with an intensity that led me to believe there were some rather ungentlemanly thoughts rolling around behind them. He licked his plump bottom lip and smiled as if he could already taste me. His head lowered, his arms squeezing me like I might run away.

I closed my eyes, unable to resist the urge to kiss him.

Hot breath blew over my mouth. His gentle lips brushed across mine like a butterfly fluttering in circles from my top lip to my bottom then back again. It wasn't quite a kiss, more a caress, but just as effective at turning me inside out. My body relaxed in his arms. A shuddered breath escaped my chest. The fabric between my thighs dampened. I tried turning around to face him, but he held me tight in place. I arched up to lock our mouths together, but he backed away, maintaining a mere whisper of a connection. I whimpered and opened my eyes.

Dean smiled, skimming his enticing lips along my jaw, then rubbing his stubble against my flushed cheeks. "I want to be sure you *really* want me when you get me," he cooed. "You seem a little uncertain."

He had no idea how certain I was. I absolutely wanted him, so much that my thighs were trembling with need, but I couldn't add him to the tally of bodies I'd used then destroyed.

A loud knock rattled the door next to us, and we both jerked to attention. I stared at the white wood, mildly distracted by Dean's body encasing mine.

"Does that mean we get in?"

I glanced up at him, then nodded, gathering my wits again. I repeated the audible code to get in.

The door eased open and a pair of red-rimmed eyes appeared around the edge, shifting from me to the sailor latched around me. "Who ya got there, Viv?"

"Frankie," I whined, rolling my eyes, "let us in." I pushed my palm against the wood and stepped over the threshold. Reaching back for my companion's hand, I urged him to follow. "This is Dean. He's with me. That's all you need to know." I smirked then stretched up, kissing the man's wrinkled cheek. The faint odor of stale alcohol radiated from his skin. Though he wasn't the most pleasant-smelling bloke in the joint, he always welcomed me like a daughter.

"Vivienne, you know you can't be bringin' any Tom, Dick, and Harry you want down here," he yelled over Dean's shoulder.

"Yeah, yeah. Where's Betty?" I tugged Dean through a dingy hallway and into a large space occupied by small tables and crowded chairs. Privileged members of Molly's secret club filled every seat. Another dozen people huddled against the walls or squeezed around the small bar.

Despite the rickety house above and the lack-luster entrance to Molly's, inside the century and a half old cellar was quite swanky. Frankie had tiled the dirt floor in a black and white checkered pattern during his younger days and layered the walls with rich mahogany planks. Royal blue linens covered every table. Brass trim gleamed from the liquor shelves behind the bar. Dim lighting created a relaxing, sensual atmosphere for the more adventurous couples, as well as the men who brought their mistresses out for a night on the town, leaving their poor, naïve wives at home. There were few rules in Molly's, one of the most important being, "What goes on underground ain't nobody's damn business."

It was no wonder Betty didn't want to settle down after working in this place. We witnessed the worst side of men down here, but Betty and I were probably the best treated gals in the joint. We did our jobs and didn't snitch or complain when Frankie allowed some of the town's riskier business and transgressions to occur under his roof. He gladly accepted the "extra dues" charged during those business meetings to help pay for care of his ill wife, May.

Frankie shouldered by Dean and me, pausing to spark up his pipe. He inhaled a deep puff and pointed to a shadowy corner next to the stage. "Over there," he said, eyeing Dean disapprovingly. "Don't you Navy boys start any shit with my friends, understand?"

Dean grinned and nodded. "Wouldn't think of it, sir."

The old man's tired gaze scanned to me. "Five's the limit, Viv."

I giggled, knowing Alan, the bartender, wouldn't hold me to Frankie's cut-off. "Whatever you say, Frankie."

He inhaled another puff from his pipe, shot Dean a look meant to intimidate, which I doubt did anything to frighten the sailor, then headed for his post at the door. He was strict about who was invited into the club and preferred clearing the newcomers himself.

Dean chuckled. "What was that about?"

"He's a bit overprotective of us girls." I pulled him toward the bar.

Alan feverishly wiped spilled spirits off the varnished surface pieced together from boards of driftwood Frankie found on the beach when he first opened Molly's. He glanced up, noticing me darting toward him, and widened his toothy grin. Before I made it to the bar, he was tipping a bottle of my favorite liquor over a short glass.

"Hi-ya, Al!" I greeted. "This here's Dean. Drinks are on him tonight." I winked, picking up the glass Alan just finished pouring, then smiled at Dean.

Allan nodded, snickering. "I see you've got your hands full with this one tonight. What'll it be for you, Mister?"

Dean smirked, cocking an eyebrow up at me. "That I do, Al." He turned his attention to the bartender. "Jim Beam, if ya have it, sir."

"Right-O." Allan bent over, reaching under the bar, and pulled out a clear bottle of burnished-gold liquid. He extracted a glass from the stack next to him, sitting it right-side up on the counter. Upturning the bottle, he poured Dean's request then served it. "We'll settle before you go."

"Thanks, Al," I chimed, snagging Dean's elbow and tugging him away. Perusing the room, I saw a couple leave their seats and disappear out the door. I led him to the table positioned near the stage. Under the low lights, we would be fairly inconspicuous among the crowd, but still have a keen view of the club from there.

Dean stepped ahead of me, pulling out one of four chairs stowed under the table. I graciously accepted, tucking my skirt against my rear and sitting like a proper lady. He lowered into the seat next to me, scooting it as close to me as possible.

"So, you work here?" Dean asked, leaning in toward me, his arm grazing mine.

My eyes lingered on the spot where we touched, imagining how good it would feel if our bodies were bare and pressed together. I swallowed the need building inside and focused on his question. "Yes, Betty insisted I take the open position when I first moved to Charleston."

He sipped on his drink, his tongue making a quick swipe across his lush bottom lip. "Where did you live before?" Steely eyes swept over my face, stopping on my mouth as I cleared my throat. I felt like I was drowning from the need he was stirring in me.

"Um, my father is a small farm owner in Spartanburg. Sells his harvest at the local markets. That's where I've lived since I was sixteen." I tore my eyes from his gorgeous face, lifting my glass to my lips and drawing in a mouthful of liquor. I gulped it down, wishing the soothing effects would take over sooner rather than later.

"And…before sixteen?" he inquired. Dean nudged me with his shoulder, urging me to continue.

"Where did you come from?" I countered. I didn't want to dredge up my history. It only made my compulsions worse.

He laughed and leaned back in his chair, putting a minimal distance between us. It was enough for me to breathe, though. I felt like I was being smothered by his heat, by the tension pulling me to him.

"Changing the subject, are we?" He whistled through his teeth, eyeing my rigid posture. "Okay." Dean leaned forward again, resting his hand next to mine. He loosened his fingers from his glass and gently rubbed his knuckles along the back of my hand.

I shivered, watching his movements for a moment before picking my drink up and taking another gulp.

"I grew up in Pennsylvania, a miner's son. Gregson and I met as boys, became best friends, and joined the Navy as soon as we could. Not much to tell, really."

My gaze roamed to Betty sitting on Lt. Gregson's lap a few feet away, their tongues buried in each other's mouth, hands groping one another's bodies like they couldn't breathe if they were separated.

I opened my mouth to make a comment, but a woman's loud cackling stopped me. I looked toward the sound, recognizing the tall, slight lady right away. Vera often accompanied the richest, most ruthless members to visit Molly's. Tonight, she latched onto a short, stocky man I hadn't seen before, a new member perhaps. By the look of his well-tailored suit, expensive pocket watch, and following goons, he had plenty of money to persuade Frankie into a membership.

The couple slowed as they approached our table. "Vivie," Vera lilted.

"Vera," I returned with a polite nod.

"This is Mr. Dultsev. He was asking about a friend who came in last week. I believe you know him…Mr. Collin."

I tilted my head and narrowed my eyes in thought. "I'm sorry, I don't think I recognize the name. Was he a patron?"

"Billy," the man barked in a thick European accent. "He goes by Billy in the states." His eyes bore into me as if he knew I had a secret about his friend.

Chapter Four

Vera nodded emphatically, looking from her man to me. "That's right, doll. Billy. Didn't I see you two huddled in the corner before your set last Friday night?"

My stomach sank. All I wanted to do was forget his name, and now someone was looking for him. This was not the first time I'd run into a sticky situation after a kill, but the urgent tone of Mr. Dultsev's voice told me he *really* wanted to find Billy.

I gulped a mouthful of my brandy, the burn settling my nervousness. "Oh, yeah," I said, pretending to suddenly remember the tall drink of water I'd bedded and offed. "He...uh...I think he went home before I got off work that night. I haven't seen him since. Sorry."

Mr. Dultsev's gaze was locked on my every movement, seeming to assess my sincerity.

"You hear that, Daddy," Vera purred, "she hasn't seen him since that night. Maybe someone drove him home. We'll ask around."

Dean cleared his throat.

Vera's attention locked onto my companion as if just realizing he was there. "Who's this charmer, Vivie?" She detached from the bulldog of a man she'd entered with and bent over the table, accentuating the bosom nearly spilling over the bodice of her rosy satin evening-gown. Her hand extended out toward Dean expectantly.

"This is Dean," I introduced in a flat tone behind the rim of my glass, then tossed back the last bit of my drink.

The man at my side stood from his seat and bowed, taking Vera's hand and kissing it. "Lieutenant Dean Vitson, Miss. It's a pleasure to meet you."

Mr. Dultsev's eagle-eyed gaze raked over Dean, his expression impassive as he considered the sailor.

My date straightened, acknowledging Vera's guest with a curt nod. "Brat."

My head jerked toward Dean, eyes widened with surprise. He apparently knew where this man was from and how to speak his language.

The gentleman's mouth curled up in a smirk. He tipped his head toward Dean, then winked at me. "I'm sorry to have disturbed your time. Have goot ev'ning." Mr. Dultsev reached out and grabbed Vera's hand, yanking her back to his side. "Come, lapochka. Let dem be. Ve find table elsewhere," he said, his words so thick with an accent I could barely understand some of them.

32

Vera giggled, snuggling her breasts against his meaty arm. The two left us, moving across the room to a vacant table, pausing to mingle with a new couple every few paces.

Though Dean's glass was just under half full, I waved my hand in the air, signaling Alan that we were ready for more drinks.

"Do you know him?" I asked, eyeing the man still standing next to me.

He watched Mr. Dultsev move away from us. When the couple settled at a table on the opposite side of the club, Dean lowered to his chair and draped his arm along the back of my seat. "No," he answered, grabbing his glass and tossing back the amber liquid in one swallow. He glanced back at Vera and her sugar-daddy, then returned his focus to me, at last.

There was a shimmer of unease in his gaze, but I ignored it and leaned into his side.

He smelled so delicious. Like a cool breeze, spicy aftershave, and salt that had imbedded in his skin from months at sea.

I nuzzled his neck, breathing him in, then slid my tongue from his collar to his earlobe, tasting his sticky skin.

A growl rumbled from his throat. "Ms. Carson, you are trying your damnedest to make me less than a gentleman."

"Well, Mr. Vitson, I never claimed to be a lady who needed a gentleman."

His gray-blue eyes peered into mine, seeming to calculate the risk I presented. I was unlike any woman he'd ever met before; he was smart to consider me carefully.

Dean moved in very slowly, stopping just before his lips touched mine.

I opened my mouth, anticipating the feel of him invading me in such a personal way, wanting to experience the sparks arcing between us when we kissed.

The sudden warmth of feather-light fingertips dragged up my right ankle. They wandered along the back of my calf, sending tingles through my body. My breath shuddered. I was engulfed in his heat, in the arm wrapped around me, in the hand traveling higher on my leg, and in his bourbon-heated breath grazing over my mouth in jagged exhalations.

His tongue reached out and skimmed my bottom lip.

I whimpered at the teasing gesture. My fingers curled around the edge of the table and squeezed, hoping the rickety slab of pine would act as an anchor to keep me from floating away in his grasp.

Slightly callused fingers grazed the back of my knee, digging in a bit deeper to massage the soft flesh. "It's so hard, trying to do the right thing with you, Vivie," he exhaled. "I really just want to take you back to the car and show you what kind of a man I really am. You have no idea what ungentlemanly things I'm thinking of every second I'm with you."

"Why wait until we get in the car? You could show me what a wild cat you are right here." I closed my mouth on his and thrust my tongue between his lush lips. The scruff of his day-old beard abraded my skin as we kissed, inciting a sweet pain to the pleasure of my exploration.

I wanted to crawl inside him, to know all his secrets.

I wanted to kill him.

He held such a quiet power over me, more than any guy before him. There was always that fascination and attraction, but with Dean, there was something else. It was a yearning to submit honestly and completely.

I couldn't let him throw me off. He was just a man after all, no different than the fools that worked to get in my panties and leave me afterward, right?

Lacing my fingers with his under the table, I guided his hand up my thigh, slipping the hem of my skirt higher than socially acceptable for most public places. For Molly's, my showing a little skin beneath the tablecloth was almost prudish.

The pressure of our fingers raking up my inner thigh, gliding over my stockings, made my breath hitch. Blood flushed my cheeks and flooded every sleeping nerve in my body, burning fiery paths throughout my limbs and torso. My senses jolted to life with the rush.

He was igniting a passion I had no control over. It was a dangerous thing when I didn't have control of my faculties.

Dean peeled his mouth away from mine, panting as we reached my thin, satin panties. He rested his forehead against mine, a low grunt escaping his chest. "You are a feisty little thing, aren't you?" A wide grin spread across his face, and he turned his hand to cup the hot flesh at the apex of my thighs.

He suddenly shifted in his chair, turning toward me more and widening his legs. "My god, I can feel how wet you are through your panties."

Before I could answer, Dean's finger pressed into my folds, trapping the satin against my most sensitive part. He slid his fingertip up and down in painstakingly slow strokes, pulling deep, throaty moans from me every time he passed over my aching bud.

I rested against my chairback, tilting my hips forward. My eyes scanned absently over the rowdy crowd dancing, chattering, and drinking around us. When my gaze landed on Dean's hungry expression, a sudden spike of pleasure shot from my pelvis outward. My nipples puckered, and my thighs clenched. Even my scalp tingled with the blaze of ecstasy growing in my core.

Slouching helplessly into the curve of Dean's chest, I held my breath and swallowed back the cry of release that racked my body.

Dean's finger slowed to a stop. He gently readjusted my soaked panties back to a comfortable position and rested his forehead against mine. "You are like dynamite in a bottle. I'm not sure I can undo the damage you've just done to me, Vivie." His eyes narrowed, searching mine for some truth he likely wouldn't find. He leaned in and kissed me softly—sweetly. He straightened my skirt over my thighs without taking his lips from me, diligent in caressing my skin along the way.

The tangible tension lingering between us only stirred me into a frenzy that much more. I wanted him with a voracious need. I wanted him inside me.

I yearned to feel the euphoria that I was sure he'd bring when I conquered his life.

He was such a strong, confident man. Overcoming him would be as sweet as muscadine wine.

Dean pulled away, his heavy gaze alive with erotic thoughts of what he'd do to me given the chance.

I licked my lips, still tasting his heady flavor. I curled my fingers over his knee and slid them upward. It was his turn to unravel in the middle of a crowded room.

His back stiffened, and his chest froze on a deep inhale. He glanced to a woman cackling in the far corner then at Alan gliding to a table three spots down from us. None of them were the wiser.

When my fingers smoothed over the bulge in his pants, he released his breath with a low groan.

It was the sexiest sound I'd ever heard. Instantly, my skin prickled with desire.

I stretched up to whisper in his ear, smiling when he shivered from my nearness. "You haven't even had a taste of the havoc I can wreak, baby. It's probably best you just forget about me now."

Dean's plump lips pulled at one corner in a sly grin. He raised the hand he'd just had under my skirt and slipped his middle finger into his mouth, sucking the tip as if it were doused in honey. "Mmm," he purred, "I don't know...if this is what havoc tastes like, I definitely want more."

I squeezed his thick, swollen cock. My lips parted on an eager breath. I fantasized about how perfectly he'd fit inside me. Not too big, not too small. I could almost feel him slipping into me, stretching me just enough to create the right amount of friction that could shatter me with one orgasm after another.

His head fell back. His eyes closed to the raucous patrons keeping Molly's alive. I watched the vein in his neck pound a rapid beat with the music blaring from the instruments on stage.

His exposed neck teased me, beckoning me to grip my other hand around his windpipe. It'd be a struggle with this one. He was so much bigger and broader than most of the men I've taken down, but the end would be well worth the challenge. He was full of passion—fire and drive that propelled him forward in life. He had a force that most people can't even comprehend once they settle into their mundane routines, carrying on with goals to be exactly like everyone else. Dean was unique, though. There was no settling with him. I had a feeling, with him, all you could do was hold on for the ride.

I tightened my grip, increasing my pace as I worked him through his carefully pressed pants. He rolled his head down, peering at my hand through a sliver of dark lashes. His fingers dug into my shoulder, urging me closer to his side. "If you keep that up, I'm going to blow my fuse right here," he panted.

"It's only fair."

His hand brushed up my arm and neck before tangling in my hair. "You smell so good. Like honey and rain." He grazed his stubble over my earlobe, sending a shiver up my spine. "You taste even better."

I shifted in my chair, pressing my thighs together. That didn't help the ache deep inside, though.

His hot breath rushed in and out, searing my cheek on the exhales. Every muscle in Dean's body tensed, his right hand clutching the edge of the table while his left arm clamped me to his side. He gritted his teeth and a muffled grunt escaped his beautiful lips. A sudden gathering of moisture dampened the fabric next to his fly. I slowed my strokes, homing in on his every shudder, each little sign of satisfaction, until his body relaxed.

He was intoxicating.

As much as I wanted to give in to my dark desires, something in the back of my mind was yelling, *Don't do it. Not him.*

CHAPTER FIVE

"You gonna sing, Vivie?" a bubbly voice asked.

I looked up to see Betty's bright smile beaming back at me expectantly.

"No. Not tonight." I nudged my chin toward the stage. "Gene's here. She's got it covered."

Betty rolled her eyes and huffed. "Don't give me no shit, Vivie. You know you're way better than her. Get up on that stage and sing us a song," she demanded with a drunken hiccup.

"You sing?" Dean bent forward, resting a forearm on the table. "Sing me a song, Ms. Vivie." He smiled, a glimmer of intrigue shining in his eyes.

I inhaled a deep breath while tidying my rumpled dress. I flipped through the many songs I usually sang in my head, settling on one that was slow and sultry.

There were nights, the really rowdy ones, that I stepped onto the stage and silenced the entire club with the first note. The nights I sang were often the busier evenings, but I always had a sense of trepidation just before taking my place on the small platform. I worried that being in front of crowds would expose me somehow, bring too much attention. However, when I was up there, the freedom I tasted was a close second to the high I felt after a kill.

Tonight, I needed that rush to distract me from Dean. I prayed it would fulfill that deep need in my belly.

Betty, Richard, and Dean all stood up, cheering me on from our table as I zigzagged around sloshed patrons toward the rear of the building. I smiled shyly, hopping onto the modest stage. After greeting the band I sang with regularly, I told them which song to play. They set into a rhythm as smooth and rich as black velvet.

Jim, my drummer, tapped out a steady rat-a-tat-tat on a worn cymbal, using the scraggly wire brush he'd had for years. Benjamin situated his lips on the mouth-piece of his sax and began a wailing cry of musical notes that filled the smoky air with just the right amount of tormented love. Waiting his turn for a few beats into the melody, Terrance finally added his bass, making my bones vibrate under strategic plucking of low-toned strings. That was my favorite. I loved feeling the music vibrate my body to the core, zapping me to life, no matter what mood I was in.

Tonight, I was in a dangerously seductive mood.

I wrapped my fingers around the mic pole, filling my lungs with the air I needed to sing. The first note of the song brewed from my diaphragm and rang against my vocal cords, creating the perfect timbre, then rose higher as it cleared my lips. The room quieted. All eyes focused on me.

A small spotlight Frankie had rigged to a beam on the ceiling shone down where I stood, blinding me from the farthest half of the club. I couldn't see Dean, but I could feel his gaze boring into me, his heat reaching across the distance and setting my body on fire.

I closed my eyes, sinking into a song about a treacherous love affair; two hearts bound together by a carnal need, yet doomed by the consuming fever of their yearning. Lifting and dropping my voice in silky tones, I drew out every emotion trapped in the song, relaying it to those watching me.

When I finished, the audience roared, hollering over an eruption of boots stomping on the floor and sharp whistles. I slowly opened my eyelids. Dean stood as still and intimidating as a mountain next to the stage with his arms crossed over his chest. Pure longing seeped from his expression.

I bowed to the audience and turned, thanking the band, before I stepped off the stage.

With our palpable heat stealing every bit of my focus away from the other people in the crammed club, Dean held out his hand, offering me help down to his side.

A clever grin tugged at one corner of his mouth. "You're just full of surprises, aren't you?" He leaned down, skimming his stubbled jaw against my cheek. "Your voice is so sweet...I'd love to hear how it sounds when you're singing my name in pleasure," he whispered.

A slow tingle rolled up my spine and radiated through my body. Snapshots of his face shifted into my thoughts, his features poised in a look of shock and fear, his mouth frozen around a choked attempt to cry *my* name. I grinded my pelvis down onto him with my hands squeezing his windpipe unbearably tight.

"There's still time for that, though. We don't have to rush, dolly." He straightened, watching my face for a response.

"I think that'd be best."

I didn't want to wait. Every anticipating impulse fluttering over my nerve endings needed to feel him inside me, filling me, and bringing me to the sharp point of release. Yet, something deep in my chest whispered as soft as a gentle breeze gliding along my skin. It said, *Not him. He's not for conquering, my dear.*

Dean nodded, likely thinking my trepidation was based on innocence, not the thoughts of a monster. "Come on. Let's find our friends. Looks like it's starting to thin out in here anyway." He nudged his chin toward a group of eight stammering to the door. Stragglers from a few smaller huddles of customers bid their "goodnights" and left as well.

I nodded, allowing him to guide me back to our table. Halfway there, we passed Mr. Dultsev and Vera. I smiled politely at the gaunt, busty woman then paused, noticing Mr. Dultsev's eyes harden when he saw me. His stormy gaze darted to Dean, locking onto him. The stout, round Russian dipped his head toward Dean in a knowing gesture. I couldn't see my sailor's expression, but I felt an urgent jerk on my hand.

We were once again in motion, hurrying to where Betty's laughter bubbled up across the room.

"What was that about?" I asked, struggling to keep up with Dean's pace.

"Nothing," he barked. "We need to go."

He gripped Lieutenant Gregson's bicep, whispering something in his ear. Gregson's eyes found Vera and Mr. Dultsev wandering toward the exit. The two men eyed the odd-looking couple until they vanished out the door.

"Let's scram, baby," Gregson urged Betty, who was eyeing him with the same suspicion I had of Dean.

She looked at me, and I shrugged. Betty grabbed her purse from the back of the chair. "Tab," she called to Al, letting him know we would clear any fees when we came in for our next shift.

"Yeah, yeah," he deadpanned, swiping a booze-stained towel over the bar.

Our men steered us out into the cool night air, up the steps, and back to the car. Their gazes constantly surveyed our surroundings, occasionally flicking at one another then scanning the shadows again.

Gregson lit a cigarette and leaned against the car, waiting patiently for Betty to unlock the passenger side door for him. She had no clue that his eyes slid over her with a genuine fondness. "Thanks, baby," he said around a billowing puff of smoke.

Betty stretched up on her tiptoes and kissed his chin in a gesture that could be one of those cutesy things couples did for the rest of their lives. She unlocked my door, then skipped around the rear of the car.

Before she reached her side, Richard slid in, lay across the seat to unlock her door, and pushed it open. An appreciative sigh blew from Betty's mouth as she lowered onto the driver's seat.

Dean placed his hand on the small of my back to urge me forward, stopping me from being the sad voyeur who longed for the love blooming between my best friend and her Lieutenant. I crawled in the car and scooted over behind Betty. Dean followed, slamming the door shut while he swept his gaze over the mostly empty street ahead of us. "Can we get this tin can going, Betty?" he asked in a mildly frustrated tone.

The two lovebirds broke free from each other's clutches. Betty glared back at Dean without a word, relaying every bit of irritation through her narrowed eyes. When she was satisfied that he understood her, she started the car, mumbling a few curse words under her breath.

"Is everything okay?" I asked, taking in Dean's stiff posture and bouncing knee.

His leg stilled. He exhaled, focusing on me for the first time since we left the club. He relaxed back into the seat, forcing his frame to loosen when he saw the concern in my eyes. "Yeah. Everything's fine. I'm sorry. I just didn't like the look of that guy is all. He...," his lips pursed, and he looked out the window, "I don't know. There was something about him."

Silence filled the space between us as we drove out of the city. Fewer and fewer lights lined the street, until finally we were driving through the pitch of night. I thought we were headed back to the boys' ship, but my insides started to churn when the headlights beamed over the familiar landmarks indicating we were going to our house.

I lurched forward, grabbing Betty's shoulder, praying I was wrong. "Where are we going?"

Her eyes flicked up to the rearview mirror, a tiny line forming above the bridge of her nose. "Home, silly." She craned her neck to see me clearer in the mirror, sensing the panic on my face. "What's wrong with you?"

I could see it in my reflection, too. She had taken guys home before, but this time there was a guy with *me*. I was usually the third wheel, always making an excuse to leave my date behind. She knew I wasn't a prude, but she didn't know to what extent. She didn't know anything about the dark compulsions that flooded my mind.

Dean leaned forward. He grabbed my hand and pulled it back, coaxing me into his side. "Don't worry. I'll sleep on the sofa."

Normally, my needs overcame my will to keep a safe distance, and I eventually gave in. I'd started on that path tonight, with Dean, but I found the control to refrain from bedding this man. Things had heated up, and there was definitely something between us, but my interests in him were different than the men I'd had before. As much as I wanted to find my pleasure in his demise, I wanted to find pleasure in his future too. Yet, somehow, all my efforts had just been thwarted by the simple act of Betty inviting them to our pad.

I didn't know if Dean sleeping on the couch would be enough to dampen my temptations.

CHAPTER SIX

"I'll get some blankets," I said nervously.

Betty and Richard barely made it into the house before they started tearing their clothes off. She squealed a quick, "Goodnight, kids," between kisses as she shoved Richard down the hall to her room. The door slammed behind them, muffling eager moans and giggles.

"I'll stay here," Dean assured, looking at the couch with disappointment.

I slipped off my shoes next to the kitchen bar, then padded my way to the other end of the house. Thankfully, mine and Bet's rooms were on opposite sides of the small one-level. Otherwise, I'd have to listen to her bed guests all the time. That would be brutally painful — being aroused more often than I already am — and more dangerous for those in my path.

Reaching for the pile of comforters on the shelf in my closet, I sensed someone behind me and spun around, dropping the blankets on the floor.

Dean spied on me from the doorway. He'd removed his uniform shirt. A tight white undershirt hugged the thick muscles shaping his chest and abdomen.

I licked my lips, my mouth suddenly feeling like I'd eaten a handful of sand. He crossed his arms over his chest and inhaled deeply, ropes of flesh bunching as he moved.

"I...I thought you were staying out there," I croaked, bending over to pick up the blankets at my feet. It was the only thing I could do to keep from throwing myself at him.

"I was," he answered, taking a step into my room, "but, I couldn't stand being away from you any longer." Stalking toward me, his eyes raked me up and down in a slow, fervid motion like he was memorizing each curve of my body.

I took a step back, pinning myself against the closet door with nowhere to go, feeling very much like a trapped animal.

I didn't want to hurt him—but, God, how I wanted to bring him to his knees in pain and pleasure.

My fingers tightened around clumps of rose-printed fabric. He stopped on the other side of the blankets. I looked up into his gorgeous eyes and bit the inside of my cheek, begging for my self-control to prevail.

Dean coaxed the comforters from my hands, smirking at my unwillingness to give them up. He set them on the vanity next to him. "Is it that bad, being near me?" He chuckled.

I shook my head, holding my breath, afraid that if I spoke or moved too much, I would lose it.

His lips parted, and he ducked his head. Warmth heated my already flushing skin.

Inhaling sharply, I smelled the faint sweetness of whiskey on his breath. The need to steal the air from his lungs overcame me.

I closed my eyes. Maybe if I didn't see him, I could pretend it wasn't happening. I could pretend I was dreaming and trick my incessant desire to cause my lovers pain into ignoring my yearning for Dean.

The long, hard length of his body pressed into me, his hands unpinning the curls at the nape of my neck. He brushed his fingers through my hair, guiding it to lay in an auburn sash over my left shoulder.

I released a strained moan when I felt the soft flick of his tongue lap between my lips. Once, twice, three times, he teased me then plunged into my mouth, tasting me and beckoning me to accept his invitation to join him in a passionate kiss.

Tilting my head back, I opened my mouth wider and stretched my tongue past his eager lips. We danced without moving our feet, giving and taking with languid, fever-inducing licks.

I curled my fingers around the pleats of my skirt, hanging on for dear life. A slight tug on my hair pulled me away from his mouth, tipping my head back to expose my neck. I grunted then smiled, enjoying the subtle challenge he was giving me.

Dean groaned. He bent down and licked a slick leisurely line from the center of my collarbones to the tip of my chin. He stared down into my eyes with a fierceness that told me he'd have me one way or another. His hand dragged down the length of my hair, following the strands over my shoulder, and tucked into the front of my bodice between my breasts.

My breath hitched as I was yanked forward. Dean whirled around me and ushered me toward my bed by the neckline of my dress. He walked behind me, his thighs forcing mine to move in quick steps until I was sandwiched between the mattress and him.

I panted like I'd just climbed a mountain. With his fingers shoved in my cleavage, the fitted cotton around my torso felt as constrictive as a corset. The rapid rise and fall of my breast grated my aching nipples against the inside of my dress, working the sensitive buds into tight points.

With one quick yank of his arm, I was bent over the edge of the bed. My cheek, chest, and stomach fell flat against my Perfectly Peach duvet.

Dean curved around me like a spoon, the heat of his hips burning me with an untamable fire that reached straight to my core. "I bet you feel as good as you taste." He ground his pelvis into my rear, his swollen cock nestling in the crease of my cheeks.

I moaned, pushing back into his up and down nudges.

Dean gathered my rumpled hair out of my face and spread it atop the bed. He kissed my ear, then my cheek, with a tenderness that contrasted the absolute control he was asserting on my body. He appeased the yearning for love and affection in me, but also gave me the dark challenge I needed.

No man had ever made me feel like this before.

He slid off my body until I could only feel his warmth on the back of my legs. Confident hands found the edges of my thigh-high stockings, snapping them from my garter before dragging them down both legs at the same time. The soft friction sent a shiver up my spine. His long fingers encircled each ankle. He slowly raked up my calves, my knees, and dug into the backs of my thighs.

My nerves tingled under his rough touch, begging for more.

A cool rush of air chilled my hot skin as Dean raised my skirt and draped it across my lower back. He gasped. His fingertips traced the band of quarter-sized black hearts on my leg. "Oh, I like these," he said appreciatively. "Do they mean something?"

I started to stand, but his hand shot out, pushing down on my back.

"Don't move," he commanded.

How ironic; he saw them as some hidden, naughty art I put on my body. Little did he know, if we kept this going, I'd be adding his mark along with the others.

I didn't even know how to explain them to him. With the others, this was all so easy. I made up some silly reason for getting the tattoo hearts, took my fill of the man, and then took his life without batting an eye—at least, not until afterwards. This cat was making everything more complicated than it already was.

When I remained silent, Dean didn't press. His hand glided over the thin silk covering my rear and squeezed my cheeks, lifting them while spreading them at the same time.

I jerked into the bed when the sensation of something small and pointed brushed down the seam of my ass and stopped over my sex. A loud inhalation sounded from between my legs, followed by a low growl. "Mmm. I can't get enough of you, Vivie. You smell fucking fantastic."

I whimpered. My insides warred with the urge to let him continue down this dark road and the foresight of stopping him while he was still alive.

His thumb stretched down to rub short strokes along my hidden opening. My panties grew wetter with every slide of his fingertip.

"You are amazing. I've never seen a gal get so wet."

Before I could respond, he hooked his thumb around the strip of fabric. The surprise of his tongue tasting me shot jolts of dizzying desire through my pelvis. I sucked in a stunned breath then exhaled it in a moan.

"Like honey and rain," he panted, his hot mouth hovering over my slippery sex. His tongue continued licking, dipping, between my folds in excruciatingly tender swipes as if I were ice cream melting on a cone.

I clutched the duvet, arching my back in a tightly strung bow. The intense flood of blood and euphoria zoomed from my toes to the top of my head, transforming my body into a humming beam of electric need.

Dean tugged my panties farther to the side then smoothed his other hand down my ass until the pad of his thumb pressed inside my wet heat. He sunk it deeper, finding a spot at the front of my pelvis that zapped a livewire through my core.

I cried out in agonized pleasure as he massaged the hypersensitive area over and over again. Velvety moisture seeped from my sex like water trickling from a crack in the dam. He was so close to breaking the wall. The right amount of pressure would fracture the confines and allow the fluid to flow as free as a waterfall.

The sudden pressure of his fingers rubbing my swollen bud thrust me over the edge. My rapid breaths caught in my throat, my eyes squeezed shut, and I gritted my teeth. My release came with a strangled groan and a body-quaking expulsion of tension.

I was the sun releasing a flare of pent energy. Unfortunately, it was never enough to lessen my threat of destruction.

The sailor slipped his thumb out of me and growled.

My orgasm spilled out in a hot gush and trailed down the slit of my lips. I shuddered when the flat of his tongue moved from my mound to my perineum in one slow sweep, catching every drop of my pleasure.

I slumped against the bed with my fingers still curled around handfuls of my blanket, panting at the shattering experience he'd given me.

Dean stood and curved around me again, whispering in my ear between ragged breaths, "I know I broke my promise, but I'm not sorry. I've been thinking about tasting you since I met you." He straightened, tugging my panties back into place, then lowered my skirt.

I pushed myself up off the bed and spun to see him gathering the guest bedding from my vanity. "What are you doing?" The words tumbled from my mouth in a whiney rush.

I wanted more. My body ached to feel him deep inside me. I needed him to satisfy this hunger before I put his soul to rest.

He paused halfway to the door. The tip of his tongue peeked out and licked his bottom lip, reminding me of how it felt when he licked *me*. A cruel, knowing grin formed on his sexy face. "I can still taste…," his words trailed off. He shook his head and squared his shoulders. "I think that's enough for tonight." Lustful steel-blue eyes stared at me for a moment, then he nodded once with resolve and moved toward the door.

I huffed out a breath of disbelief and hurried to him. Grabbing his arm, I turned him around and shoved him into the wall. He dropped the blankets. Dean's strong hands gripped my waist and yanked me toward him as I crashed my lips into his. Our mouths twisted and sucked, feverishly trying to deepen our connection. The sweet burn of his touch scouring up my back, along with the sting of his fingers tangling in my hair and pulling, forced me to moan.

I reached down between us and found his cock straining against his pants. My fingers worked to undo his buttons, freeing him as we kissed. He was so perfect. Soft as suede. Thick, and long enough to nestle deep inside me where he could glide over all the right triggers.

Breaking our kiss, I stumbled back a step and tried to slow my breathing. I licked my lips, reaching my hands under the hem of his shirt. Scraping my nails along the ripples of his stomach, I pushed it up until I could see most of his torso. He hissed in a breath, grinding his teeth from the painful pleasure.

Bending down, I placed a light peck above his naval. I grinned when the gentle friction of my chin nudging the tip of his bound erection elicited a throaty moan. I traced the defined line of his abdomen with my tongue, stopping an inch or two higher each time to bite or suck on his tanned flesh. Once I reached his chest, I shifted to his right side and swirled my tongue around his nipple. He exhaled another sweetly agonized sound. Maneuvering his shirt up a bit further, I caught a glimpse of two blood-red points hiding under the fabric.

I stopped, the hint of something familiar tugging at my thoughts. My brows pulled together. I shoved the shirt up. Just beneath his right collarbone, I found crimson and black ink staining his skin in the shape of a star.

My voice came out shrill and full of concern. "What is this, Dean?"

I'd seen this tattoo three times now. I couldn't dismiss it as a coincidence any longer.

Chapter Seven

"What?" Dean narrowed his eyes, gauging my abrupt change in mood.

"This," I said, stabbing my finger at the tattoo on his chest. "Where did you get this?"

He chuckled. "Do we have to talk about this now?" His arms looped around my waist and pulled me closer. He kissed my neck. "I'd rather do more of this." He nipped at my earlobe.

I wanted to forget I even saw the damn symbol and allow him to keep putting his mouth on me, but I couldn't. There was no way I could be so careless.

I locked my hand around his jaw and squeezed hard enough to get his attention. He stilled. I forced his head back. "Where did you get it?"

He huffed out a breath of frustration. His jaw tensed under my fingertips as he thought about his answer a little longer than I was comfortable with.

What was he hiding?

"Nowhere. It's just something stupid I did as a kid."

I shook my head. "No, I've seen this before." My eyes shifted down to the star again. "Don't lie to me, Dean. I need to know what it means, and who did it."

He yanked his shirt down, snatching it from my grip, then pried my fingers from his jaw. Massaging his chin for a moment, he eyed me suspiciously. "You saw this star? You're sure?"

I nodded, placing my hands on my hips.

"You've been hanging with the wrong people then."

"Well, I'm here with you, aren't I? You don't seem so bad," I smirked.

"If you only knew, Ms. Vivie." Dean adjusted himself through his pants then began buttoning his shirt. "I think we're done here tonight. Have a good evening, Vivienne." He bent down, picked up the crumpled blankets, and stood, pausing to say, "I truly enjoyed your company." A smile curved his lips as he turned to leave.

In a split second, flashes of the many ways this night could've ended, including me killing him after mind-blowing sex and letting him walk out that door to live another day, played in my mind. Somehow, I managed to let him go. We were intimate with each other, but not so intimate that I'd reached my point of no return. Where that was with him, I wasn't quite sure, but I hoped he would leave in the morning and never give me the chance to find out.

After Dean left my room, the air seemed to cool. The atmosphere was thick with an uncomfortable feeling of something left open-ended, begging for my attention. I ignored it, though. I couldn't afford to lose myself with him. Dean could avoid telling me what the tattoo meant for now, but eventually, I'd need to know the truth. If I killed him and he was connected to my former victims with the same tattoo, I'd only leave more evidence for someone to link back to me.

I'd managed to escape Atlanta without notice, before the cops learned of my involvement with the men I killed there. I didn't want to leave Charleston so soon. I loved living here. It was the closest thing to home I'd found since leaving my father's farm. I was close to Dad, but not so close that I'd drag him into any backlash from my bad impulses.

Mulling over the possible excuses for Dean's ties to Billy and Jacob, I unzipped the back of my dress and shoved it over my excessively round rump, leaving it on the floor in a puddle where it landed. I threw back the covers and climbed into bed, yanking the duvet back on top of me.

I replayed the details of each experience, scrutinizing every detail to make sure I left nothing behind that pointed to me. I recalled what I wore those evenings, verifying that I had all my clothing and jewelry on me when I left. No one would be able to tell it was me by the marks I left on Billy's neck, or by the thin puncture wound in Jacob's chest where I'd stabbed him with the stiletto knife I kept in my garter on occasion.

To my knowledge, none of the men had families. We talked about that in our mindless chit-chat before going back to their places. And, until last night, I thought none of them had friends tagging along with them. That would be another loose end I'd have to watch out for.

Was Dean one of Billy's friends? Had they gotten those tattoos together? It didn't seem likely. He didn't seem to have any idea who Vera was asking about at Molly's.

Regardless, who would believe a woman could cause such violent deaths?

Staring into the low gloom of moonlight bathing my room, my thoughts wandered from the heinous crimes I'd committed and homed in on Dean. The way he moved. The heat of his body pressed against mine. The feel of his tongue exploring me. He was right down the hall, sleeping on the couch. I could go to him right now. I could take off all my clothes and go to him, finishing what we started.

The need was nearly unbearable, but the risk was too great.

My eyelids fluttered closed. Thinking of his fingers and mouth devouring me, I fell asleep.

The storm winds kicked ocean spray over the railings of the tottering boat. The great sails stretched around the blows, steering us in an uneven path through raging waves.

"Tighten the ropes, Vivie," Daddy called. I focused on the panic in his eyes then looked for Mama. I couldn't find her through the commotion of water breaching the boat and the pitch-black bleeding in between flickers of Daddy's lantern.

My small hands caught the rope whipping the deck and tugged on it, but I was too light to keep it taut. The sail swung across the boat, lifting me with it. I cried out, gripping the rope with what strength I could muster. My palm slid along the frayed fibers, biting into my tender flesh and burning until the end of the rope broke free from my grasp. I slammed onto the planked floor, screaming and holding my hands.

"Mommy," I yelled in a shrill child's voice. "Mommy, I can't see you." I searched the bow and found Daddy grabbing the stray sail. He wound the tie around a giant hook. The boat jerked. My small body slid into the railing. I looked up through tears and rain, hoping Daddy was okay. He was stumbling toward the big wheel at the back of the vessel again.

Suddenly, I felt Mommy's warm arms wrapping around me. She had crouched down beside me without me noticing and scooped me into a tight hug.

"Listen to your father, kukla. He'll protect you. Be careful who you trust, they have eyes everywhere." She squeezed me tighter and kissed my forehead. A sad smile spread across her beautiful face. "I love you," she whimpered, sniffling as tears mixed with the rain and dripped down her cheeks.

"I love you too, Mommy. Don't go," I squealed, digging my fingers into her arms when she unwound them from me. She pried my hands off her, then stood and turned away from me. I scrambled to follow her but kept getting tossed by the bouncing boat. I yelled at Daddy, trying to get his attention over the roaring storm, but he was too busy fighting to steady the boat.

Mommy wavered back and forth, pounding her hip into the gold rail as she trekked to the bow. When she finally made it to the tip of the vessel, her head turned, and she peered back at me for a moment. Mommy smiled.

My hands and feet slipped on the deck's drenched surface, slowing my progress to reach her. Something felt wrong. Mommy wasn't acting right. I felt like she was saying goodbye.

I screamed, reaching my hand out to skim the back of her soaked dress. Her body leaned forward and gracefully tipped over the front edge of the boat like a swan diving.

I sucked in a deep, scared breath. Mommy didn't have a vest on. She was supposed to wear a vest when there was a storm. Why didn't she have a vest on?

Stretching over the railing, I looked down into the cool, choppy ocean and saw the faint ghostly outline of her skin glowing against the black waters. She was still smiling, her eyes staring up at me, as she sunk deeper until I couldn't see her anymore.

"Get up, sleeping beauty!" Betty chimed before bouncing onto my bed.

"What time is it?" I groaned, pulling the covers over my head to hide from her bubbly greeting and the sunlight spilling into my room.

"It's noon. We need to run some errands, so get that fat rump of yours up and moving." The sting of her hand slapping my right butt-cheek earned another groan. She bounced up and down on my mattress a few more times to make sure I was completely awake.

"Are the guys here?" I whispered.

"No," she whispered back with a giggle. "They were gone before I got up. Rich left me a note saying they had to report back to the ship pretty early. They were going to take a taxi there, I think."

"Did he say anything about them seeing us again?" I wanted to know, but the slight chance that the answer would be yes had my nerves on alert. It would be easier to just forget about Dean and let him move on with his life, which he wouldn't have if he'd stayed with me last night.

"I don't know. Rich said they were supposed to be heading out to sea today. He said he'd find me when they came ashore next time." Bet's voice was quiet. She clearly liked this cat, but she would get over him soon enough, and then he'd end up just another memory of someone she had some fun with one time. At least, I hoped that was the case.

I peeked out from under the blanket, catching Betty's backside sauntering out of my room with a bit more sway than usual.

"Richard must have done you right last night," I remarked when she was out of sight. My mind instantly thought of Dean and how I wanted him to do *me* right.

Huffing a breath of frustration, I threw my blankets off and sat up in the bed. I combed my fingers through my disheveled hair. It was too damn early for a night-owl like me.

With a lousy effort to stand upright, I pushed off the mattress and leaned over to grab my robe off the footboard. Yawning, I tied the satin tie around my waist and eyed the bold green A-line halter dress hanging my closet. I yanked it from its hanger, mad that I even had to get dressed in the first place. It was going to be a rough day. After plucking some under garments from my drawers, I padded to the bathroom across the hall.

The sounds of dishes clinking in the kitchen told me Betty was making her usual breakfast: eggs, toast, and waffles. While the rest of the world had been up for hours, it was normal for us to get up at this time and have breakfast for lunch. Our odd schedule came with working late hours at Molly's.

I turned on the water and slipped out of my robe. As I stepped into the tub, the first splashes of hot water burned my chilled skin, but it soon became comfortable. I slid the glass door closed behind me and stood under the stream, closing my eyes as the water washed away the impurities sticking to my skin.

Flashes of Dean's face appeared in my mind. The smell of his salty skin was so vivid, it was like he was in the shower with me. The taste of whiskey in his kiss had me licking my lips, wanting more. I lathered soap in my hand and slid it over my neck, along my collarbones, then around each of my puckering nipples.

His hands were so commanding. I imagined how firm his touch would be if I let him have complete control of me. My hands squeezed my heavy breasts before sliding down the slight roundness of my belly and into the patch of curls at the apex of my thighs.

Thinking about the way his fingers applied pressure, I dipped my middle finger into the slit of my sex and began a slow, steady rhythm to pleasure. Visions of his head buried between my legs, his tongue working me into a lightning strike of ecstasy, fueled every stroke that quickly brought me to a panting, yet meagerly satisfying, release.

It would have to be enough for now.

The Phone Call

"Hey, I'll be right back," I said to Rich after spotting a blue phone booth across the street.

"What's with you, man? We gotta get back," he whined, stopping to watch me jog to the booth.

I heard him exhale in frustration behind me and smiled. "It'll just take a minute," I called over my shoulder.

Squeezing in the booth, I retrieved the slip of paper from my pocket and unfolded it. I picked up the receiver, waited for the operator to answer, then fed the phone my dime. "Yeah, can you connect me to an Ivan Markow in New York City, please?"

"Hold, please," the lady instructed in a nasally voice.

I waited patiently, listening to a sequence of dings and clicks.

With my hand holding the phone against my chin, I inhaled the sweet smell of Vivienne lingering on my fingers. My dick ached. She'd tasted like Heaven and Hell at the same time. Her body surrendered to my touches, whether her mind wanted to or not. I would have to be careful with her. It was so easy to see her innocent side—all that charm wrapping around the frenzy of danger swirling inside her. I sensed it like heat radiating off her skin, but it only drew me in more. I just wanted to stand closer to the fire. I didn't care if I got burned.

"Da?" a deep baritone spoke on the other end of the line.

"Ivan?"

"Da."

"Tell Mr. Laskin that he can tell his bosses I've found her."

A moment of silence.

"Did you do it, yet?"

Guilt crept into my heart. I didn't want to do what they asked, but I couldn't let my family down. They'd been through too much. We'd come too far and worked too damn hard to break what ties with these bastards we could.

"Not yet. He's gotta promise that, when I do this, we're done. The dues are paid, and we are free. They'll be none of this coming back after years have passed and asking for another *favor*."

Another moment of silence.

"Done."

The line died, and I hooked the receiver on its base. I turned, eyeing Rich as he leaned against a storefront with his foot propped on the brick behind him. He smiled and winked at a girl passing. Her poodle skirt, pink scarf, and neat ponytail screamed naivety. When she giggled, but continued on her path, he ogled the back of her skirt, no doubt imagining what was underneath.

Rich liked to look, but I knew him better than he knew himself. He was stuck on Betty and wouldn't jingle another dame's bell until he was sure there was nothing between them.

I bit my bottom lip, folded the paper with Ivan's name on it, and placed it back in my pocket.

How was I going to tell my best friend that I was going AWOL, and not give him a good reason? He'd willingly stay behind to help me with whatever problem he thought I had, no questions asked. That was just the kind of man he was—tough on the outside and soft as cotton candy on the inside. I couldn't tell him it was to murder a woman. I had to think of something that would assure him I'd be okay without his help.

Crossing the street, I prepared the lie I was going to deal my best friend.

Chapter Eight

I finished washing then dressed, applied my makeup in various shades of pink, and twisted my hair into a low bun. Plucking my favorite emerald pin from my jewelry box, I fixed the coil of curls into place, careful not to cut my skin with the custom-made bladed edges. I always adorned myself with hidden weapons; you never knew when a gal would need a little extra help.

"I'm ready when you are," I told Betty from her bedroom door. She was fastening the last strap of her garter.

"All set," she said, lowering her leg from a high-back chair. She smoothed her navy pencil skirt down over her narrow hips and grabbed the red clutch off the foot of her bed.

We spent the next few hours buying groceries, paying bills, and shopping at Maude's Boutique in town.

Later that night, we waited in Bet's car until Frankie drove by in his Black Cherry Red Studebaker. He waved as he turned left, taking the street that ran behind Molly's. The two of us got out of the Hudson and dashed across the road.

I slowed, feeling a tingle between my shoulder blades like I was being watched.

"You okay?" Betty asked, her brows pulled together with concern.

My gaze scanned over the sidewalks on either side of the road, assessing each man and woman passing by, but no one seemed to even notice I was alive. "I'm fine," I said, sweeping the thin flow of pedestrians one last time before following her into the alley beside the barbershop.

Frankie was waiting for us at Molly's door. He stared up at the darkening purple sky, twirling a ring of keys around his index finger. "Looks like it's gonna rain, girls. You got the roof up on that old gasser, Betty?"

"Yes, Frankie," she answered, stretching up to kiss the older man on his cheek.

I repeated the gesture and trailed into the dark underground business behind Betty, flicking on the lights over the bar.

We began taking chairs down off the tables, slicing fruit for the cocktails, and helping the band set up for their gig that night.

"You g'on chirp fo' us tonight, Ms. Vivienne?" Benjamin asked in his heavy Cajun accent, then shot me a gummy grin.

"Maybe, Bennie. We'll have to see where the night takes us, won't we?"

Benjamin nodded, licking his plump, ebony lips and blew a hard breath into his saxophone.

The seats started to fill around nine o'clock. Al worked fast at getting our orders ready while Betty and I tended to our tables. It was a Saturday night, so we could expect the place to be packed by ten, and the tips made tonight should pay rent for the month.

By eleven, Gene's high-pitched crooning had just ended another song, and she announced an intermission. Al looked at me pointedly and nudged his chin toward the stage, requesting I take a turn on vocals. I glanced around at the filled tables, making sure everyone's glass was full, and then eyed the men chattering among themselves on the platform. Jim raised his gaze, noticing me watching them. He waved his hand for me to join them.

I took off my apron and laid it on the end of the bar. Straightening my halter tie and the ruffles of my skirt, I wandered between the tables toward the platform. After stepping up to take my place behind the mic, I nodded to the guys and waited for the music to start. The measured thump of Jim's drum accompanied by the methodical plucking of Terrance's bass cued me to begin. I recognized what song they were playing as soon as the melody began.

We often stayed long after Molly's closed, practicing well into the morning hours. I knew every piece they played. They were all single, their lives committed to music, and they loved hearing me sing. We all enjoyed our time together, creating stories told through magical notes that floated through the air like feathers on a breeze. It was just as much an escape for me as it was for the boys.

Tonight, they chose a song that I had recently shared with them from my own journal. We hadn't rehearsed it long, but they seemed to have the beat down. I took in a deep breath and exhaled a low, velvety note then sang the words like a prayer.

Find me freedom,

When all is lost,

Find me freedom,

At any cost.

Bring me love,

Bring me light,

Forget my soul is dark as night...

I sang each word with the begging misery that had encouraged me to write them. The room quieted, listening to me attentively while I poured out my hopes and fears. This was the first of my many written songs I'd sang outside of the confines of my room. For the next three minutes, I lost myself in the whining sax, sorrowful bass, and pounding drum. When the last note silenced, the room bloomed to life with a cacophony of whistles and cheers that jarred me back to reality.

Jim and Benjamin clapped behind me. Terrance didn't speak much, but he managed a "nice" and tipped his newsboy cap at me.

I smiled at the band, grateful for the chance to spread my wings, then left the stage. As I moved through the bundle of people standing to greet me and tell me how much they enjoyed my performance, a shadowy figure standing by the bar drew my eye. Hanging lights above the bar gleamed off his dark rain-slickened hair, giving it an almost blue hue. My heart sank.

He was supposed to leave. Why was he still here?

With my attention fully on Dean, I hurried through the crowd toward him. The hunger in his eyes was magnetic. He tore his gaze from me when Al slammed a shot down on the bar next to him. Throwing back the liquid in one hard swallow, he returned his focus to me. Dean squared his shoulders and licked his lips, taking one step in my direction before freezing.

A sweaty hand snagged my wrist, and I jolted to a stop.

"Ms. Carson," a voice growled. "Dat was some show you put on," the man said in a dense accent.

I pulled against his grip, but he didn't let loose. "Thank you," I said, glaring at him. "Is there something I can get you, Mr. Dultsev?" It was hard, but I was trying to be polite and not cause a scene.

He chuckled, his belly jiggling with the laughter. The faint smell of vodka reached my nostrils. I stared into his bloodshot eyes, waiting for an answer, still pulling my arm under his tight hold. "No." He jerked my arm to his meaty chest, causing me to stumble into him. His foul breath grazed my earlobe. "I know you offed my Billy, bitch. I will have your head on a platter before the week is up."

I straightened and stared down into his eyes, searching for certainty in his expression.

"I don't know what you think happened, sir," I gritted out, "but, I didn't do anything to Billy." The grim look on his face told me he knew I was lying, but I wouldn't back down. Until he had solid proof, no one would believe him.

"Vykhodit'," Dean growled behind me.

Startled, I glanced over my shoulder. His eyes were clouded with fury, his nostrils flaring.

"Get off. *Now*," he commanded.

The band of pressure around my wrist loosened. I clenched my fist at my side, resisting the urge to rub the soreness Mr. Dultsev left on my skin—and to punch him in the nose.

"Well, well. It's the American sailor. Did you forget vhere you come from, little fishy?" Mr. Dultsev chortled, turning up his nose at Dean. "I imagine your parents vill do vell to remind you, little fishy." He ran a white-coated tongue over his teeth then made a disgusting sucking sound. "I thought you vere to take care of your bus'ness and leave today?" The Russian eyed me for a moment then narrowed his eyes at Dean. "Perhaps, someone else vill take care of your bus'ness for you."

Dean stiffened, radiating anger so palpable it forced me to lean away from him. He inched closer to me. His fingers entwined with mine, guiding my hand and body behind him. He was trying to protect me. Little did he know, he was the one needing protection.

Mr. Dultsev silently assessed Dean, his black eyes roaming over his posture. He glanced at me, the corner of his mouth lifting in a sly grin. "Until nex' time, Ms. Carson." He barreled past us, shoving Dean back a step with his round belly.

Dean watched him join Vera at a neighboring table and insist it was time to go. Their eyes met one last time before Vera and the Russian exited the club. His body instantly relaxed.

I slid my hand from his and headed toward the bar. I snatched my apron up, fumbling to put it back on. My hands shook from fear and anger, making it hard to tie the strings at my back, so I settled on a sloppy knot.

Strong arms reached around me, latching onto the edge of the bar, trapping me inside Dean's cloud of heat. I twisted around and peered up into his eyes.

"Are you okay?" he asked, his gaze dropping to my lips.

My mouth was suddenly dry. He looked at me like he could devour me right here in front of everyone.

"I'm fine," I croaked, raising my hand to brush a fallen curl from my brow. Dean stopped me, locking my sore wrist in his fingers. He brought the underside of my wrist to his parted lips and kissed it. The warm, damp sweep of his tongue caressing the bruising flesh over my pulse point sent shivers up my spine. I stifled a gasp as he kissed and licked me again.

"You're fine, huh?" he whispered, placing my hand on his chest. "Well, I'm not. I can't think of anything but you. How you smell," he leaned in and inhaled, sniffing my hair, "how you taste." His tongue swept out, gliding across my upper lip. A low groan rumbled in his throat.

"Why are you here, Dean?" I whimpered, closing my eyes to hide the growing need in my depths.

"Order up," Al yelled from somewhere behind the bar.

Dean shot an irritated glance over my shoulder, which I guessed was for Al's impatient reminder. He returned his attention to me and bent down, stopping just before he reached my lips. "I came for you."

His body pressed into mine, heating me like a furnace built to disintegrate every fiber of who I was, rendering me into nothing more than a pile of raw, wrecked ashes.

"Vivie?" Al called in the worried tone he gets when giving me an out from the occasional men that groped on me.

"I need to see you tonight," Dean said, ignoring the barkeep.

"I don't think that's a good idea." It was true. Meeting him was a bad idea—from the very start. I wished I'd never laid eyes on him. Then, maybe I wouldn't feel the jumble of emotions urging me to open myself to him and to surrender, or the compulsion to invite him into my dangerous web and watch him suffer from my venom. "I have to go. I have tables waiting." I squeezed from between him and the bar, picking up the tray full of drinks at the end of the counter.

Dropping off a Bramble Sour and a Scotch on the rocks at table five, I noticed Dean walking out the door. A part of me relaxed, thankful that he'd given up, yet another part of me cracked—an added thin fracture in the armor that held me together, that kept me safe…kept me caged. One day, my shell would crumble, and all the ugly would spill out, ravaging anyone who crossed my path.

Chapter Nine

The first time I saw someone die was...well, they've all kind of blurred together in a terrifying mess of bodies piling in my trail. I know I was young, though.

Sometimes, I can't tell the difference between those I've murdered in my dreams, which I've had nightmares about since before my mother died, and the first few boys I barely remembered from my teenage years.

Many of my darker memories as a girl played in my mind like a movie, detached in a way that they felt like someone else's life.

But something about this guy...he reminds me of that first kill, the one I barely remember. I'm not sure what it is about him that pulls on the thread of that particular memory buried in the recesses of my mind, but there's an intriguing familiarity that speaks to me.

Betty and I closed Molly's a couple of hours after Dean left. It took all the energy I had to focus on preparing drinks and delivering them until, finally, the last member went home. I mindlessly worked through the tasks of wiping tables, sweeping, and stacking chairs. My body vibrated with the desire Dean riled up from my core—sensual and destructive.

I patted Al on the back and smiled, passing behind him to stack the last tray on a pile he kept next to the sink. I needed to be alone, I needed to find someone who could unleash this tightness in my belly, so I told Betty I would meet her at home and set out for a stroll through darkness.

As I came down Cramer Street, *this* man, a patron I'd seen at the bar earlier, approached me from across the road.

He'd ogled me all night. I hoped he'd have enough balls to seek me out and climb into my web when I was by myself. To make sure he knew I was interested, I'd flirted shamelessly, leaning over until my bosom nearly fell out of my dress, batting my eyelashes, and licking my lips provocatively.

It seemed my wiles worked like a charm.

"Hiya," he greeted in an excited tone. "Aren't you the gal that sang down at Molly's?"

Yeah, there was definitely something about him that reminded me of my first kill. Perhaps it was his overly-spiced cologne.

I nodded, smiling politely. He followed me another block, talking about how pretty I was and how much he liked my voice when I sang.

"Do you mind if I walk ya home?"

I stopped and spun, facing him, considering how much I needed a release, how trapped I felt in my own body. "What's your name?"

"Oh, my. Where are my manners? I'm sorry. Name's Stuart. Stuart Callihan." He thrust his hand toward me and waited for me to shake it. The yellow streetlight highlighted the hint of copper in his shiny hair. His pale features weren't particularly handsome, but pleasant nonetheless.

I surveyed the empty street around us. "Do you have a family, Stuart?"

His toothy grin widened. "I do, but I stay away from them as much as possible. I'm the black sheep of the family, if ya know what I mean." He winked.

"I'll bet you are," I purred, taking his hand and leading him into a garden square around the corner.

We entered the quaint courtyard through a towering trellis covered in purple swirled Wisteria vines. A waist-high brick wall fenced in the modest patch of grass and garden. It felt as though we were secluded from the rest of the world. Peony bushes lined the wall, decorating the uneven bricks with hordes of large white flowers. Tall oaks leaned into the space from outside, creating curtains of drooping branches and Spanish moss that separated us from any outsiders passing by. I tugged him along the yard stones leading to a bench tucked in a gathering of giant Magnolia trees and rose bushes.

Stuart followed as if I were taking him to a present.

I glanced over my shoulder and grinned at the sparkle of excitement lighting his green eyes. He made it too easy. That raging need that was flaring in my core since I met Dean sparked into a full blaze of lust and cruel intention. It wasn't a lust for Stuart, but he would do for now.

"Wow, this is some place. I've walked past this block quite a few times this week and didn't know this was here." His gaze roamed over the numerous plants surrounding us in a cove of foliage. "A person could get lost in here," he said, witlessly eating the bait I was feeding him.

"That's the idea," I murmured.

He jerked my hand. I looked back, seeing Stuart stumble on a loose slab of stone. He quickly righted himself, avoiding a spill to the ground, then his cheeks turned the color of beet juice.

"Guess I should pay more attention where I'm walking." He smiled apologetically.

Too easy.

I stopped in front of the bench and thought how beautifully crafted the driftwood seat and backing was. What a lovely setting this was for such a horrific act.

You could stop now. It's not too late, a voice whispered in the back on my mind.

Stuart gladly stepped toward me as I invited him to come closer. My hands looped around his neck. I stretched up just enough to reach his mouth with mine and kissed him. He was a gentle kisser, shy almost. Too chaste for what I was craving, but sweet.

I spun us around and moved forward so the back of his legs were close to the bench then slid my hands down to his chest and gave a light shove. He plopped down onto the seat, his bright green eyes darkening with the fever I saw in my victims every time they realized they were about to get lucky with me.

Reaching to the back of my neck, I slowly untied the halter on my dress. He sucked in a deep breath as I guided the two pieces covering my chest down around my waist. The night air skimmed over my nipples, hardening them to tight points.

Stuart's eyes widened, and his mouth dropped open. "Wow…"

He focused on my heavy breasts as I leaned over him and unbuckled his belt, popped open his button, and dragged down his zipper. His chest rose and fell with rapid, excited breaths. He looked like a snake hypnotized by a flute, his gaze glued to the bouncy movement of my breasts.

I hiked my dress up and settled one knee beside his left thigh then grabbed the back of the bench and lifted my other knee to straddle his lap. I lowered myself onto his wide spread legs and giggled. My God, he might have a heart attack before I get the chance to kill him. "You okay, Stuart?"

His eyes bolted to my face, and he licked his lips, nodding. "Yep," he breathed. "You're just…so damn beautiful." His small hands wrapped around my waist and slid up my ribs. Gooseflesh rippled over my skin. His touch was warm and soft.

The torturous throbbing began between my thighs. Moisture dampened my panties. The cool breeze counteracted the extreme heat radiating from my pussy and sent a shiver up my spine. My nipples hardened into aching peaks.

Stuart's mouth latched onto my right breast, engulfing the tip in hot wetness. His tongue swirled around my nipple and flicked it a few times before sucking hard then releasing it with a soft pop.

I moaned my pleasure. I almost felt sorry for him. I didn't want to kill him, but if not him, the next cat that came along would meet a more gruesome fate than Stuart. The longer the urge boiled, the worse it was when unleashed.

The sweet, lemony fragrance of Magnolias filled my nose as I arched into Stuart, delivering him my other breast. I ground my pelvis against him. Through layers of clothing, his hard flesh rubbed between my folds, strengthening the frenzy twisting inside me.

Stuart's mouth worked on my nipple as I started unbuttoning his shirt. I yanked his collar back, dragging the plaid fabric off his shoulders.

No need for that to get messy. It'd only be more evidence to hide.

I hissed in a sharp breath when Stuart's teeth grazed over my sensitive skin. Licking my lips, I leaned back and smiled, letting him know I approved of a little pain with my pleasure.

A slow grin pulled at his thin lips. "So sexy," he groaned. "So soft." His fingers dug into the fleshy curves of my hips, forcing me to grind harder on his stiff cock.

My fingers raked over his shoulders and down his chest.

I froze, my smile fading.

"What is it?" Stuart asked, his brows cinching together. "Everything okay?"

I nodded distractedly. The pads of my fingers traced over the black outline of a red, six-pointed star drawn on his left ribs. The tattoo was surrounded by a woman's portrait and a black rose bound in barbed-wire.

Stuart grabbed my wrist, clamping his hand tight around my bones. "This could have gone a lot different," he said with a slight accent — one that he hadn't had before. "We could have had a good time first. You've ruined that now." My stomach churned from the familiarity of his brogue. "We could have had a good fuck before I slit your throat." He and Mr. Dultsev shared the same rough inflections.

My eyes narrowed, and I gritted my teeth. Stuart had lost all of the shy, boyish charm and morphed into a determined killer. He and I shared that same glimmer of violence; it was clear in his devious eyes now.

His grip tightened around my wrist and, as I moved to get the stiletto I kept in my garter, he snagged my other hand. My fingertips brushed the small dagger, and it slipped from the confines of my undergarment, tumbling to the ground.

His lips pulled back into a scowl. "No, no," he commanded, "I'll have none of that tonight, suka. I know what you did to Billy, and I won't let you put me in the grave before we get our revenge."

A rustling in the Magnolia tree behind Stuart snared my attention. I stiffened, preparing to jump off him at the first chance I got and shield myself from whoever was lurking in the trees.

Before I could respond, the silvery tip of a knife pierced through the front of Stuart's throat. Blood seeped from the seam, pouring down his chest. His hands dropped from my wrists and flopped onto my thighs.

My chest heaved air in and out—not out of fear or disgust, but excitement. I bit my lower lip, my awareness of Stuart's cock still hard beneath me. I rocked over him one time, straining against the need to climax.

Branches parted behind the bench, and I looked up into stern blue eyes and an angry expression.

A shudder rolled through my body, magnifying the brutal sensitivity toying with my senses.

"Dean," I exhaled.

His severe gaze examined the corpse I straddled then drank in my flushed cheeks, panting mouth, and bare breasts.

"He was gonna hurt you," he mumbled in a gruff voice.

I nodded. "It seems he was."

Dean lifted the blade in his hand, studying the crimson streaking it. He pursed his lips and tugged on the shirt pinned between the bench and Stuart's back.

I watched him clean the blood off his knife with the plaid swatch. His hand was steady, his dark features a bit troubled, but overall, he appeared calm, considering he'd just killed a man.

"We need to get you out of here." His eyes did a quick study of the open area in the center of the garden. "They'll be coming to find him soon."

"Who will, exactly?" Nearly every move he made had me wanting him more. My pussy throbbed, my body begged for his touch. I glanced down at the slowing stream of blood coating Stuart's torso. He never would have satisfied the yearning Dean stirred in me. I realized now, he was a poor attempt to fend off an untamable inferno. Still, I was disappointed I didn't get to do the dirty work.

Dean bent over and lifted his pant leg, returning his knife to a holster fastened around his ankle. He stood and focused back on me.

I could almost feel the heat of his eyes gliding over my breasts.

He trampled through the flowers planted around the bench and moved in behind me. His big body curled around me as he reached for the ties of my dress.

I closed my eyes and leaned back into him, inhaling his ocean scent, welcoming the feel of him against me.

His fingers grazed over my tingling skin, coaxing a moan from me. The low growl rumbling from his chest vibrated across my shoulders. I opened my eyes, noticing the tinge of red soaking into my skirt.

Dean finished tying my dress back into place then slipped his hands under my arms and scooped me up. When my heels touched the ground, I took in the sight before me. Stuart's head lulled back, a sliver of skin opened just below his Adam's apple. Dark red covered his chest and stomach like a grim-looking bib. A veil of blood camouflaged the red ink of his star tattoo.

Firm hands wrapped around my upper arms and spun me around. "We have to go. Now," Dean barked. "They'll be looking for you."

"He has the same tattoo. Why, Dean?" I stumbled after him across the well-manicured lawn.

His tall, muscular body stopped sharply, his shoulders drooping the slightest amount. He didn't turn to look at me though, only waited for me to catch up behind him. With an exasperated sigh, he said, "Please, just get in the damn truck. I'll fill you in later. Right now, I'm trying to keep our body count to a minimum." Dean's voice sounded quiet and defeated.

He disappeared under a trellis at the opposite side of the garden from where Stuart and I had entered. I trailed behind him, glancing back at our victim's corpse one last time.

The Turning Point

Fucking, Laskin, I thought, stalking back to the truck. *Fucking, Laskin. He never told me there were other players in the game.*

I glanced down at the blood on my hands and grimaced. Popping the truck door open, I reached behind the seat and retrieved the old rag I'd seen Gary stuff there before I asked him to borrow the automobile. I wiped off the sticky mess as best I could.

The way my blade felt slipping into that man's spine and neck replayed in my mind. It's not like he was the first person I'd killed, but it had been awhile. I'd promised myself that this life was in my past. I'd killed to get my family away from crime and inner-city wars, and I'd taken many souls down before I decided enough was enough, but my stomach was riling with disgust and anger.

I chucked the rag back in the truck and spotted Vivienne marching toward me. She'd opted to follow. If she knew who I was, she would have run the other way.

Her skin was accentuated with a deep rose, flushed from adrenaline. Heavy breaths pushed her lush breasts tight against her dress before they fell again in an exhale.

God, she was gorgeous.

My gaze fell to the red stain marring the hem of her shamrock-colored dress. Where most women would break down and likely faint by the sheer gruesomeness of our situation, Vivienne seemed excited. I narrowed my eyes, trying to see through the alluring exterior. Could she really be as dangerous as Laskin said? Could she have killed his men?

Without a word, she jerked open the truck door, hopped onto the seat, and slammed the door shut. Her hazel eyes focused on the empty road ahead. I could fall victim to those eyes alone. Sometimes they were a bluish hue; other times, they were a meadow-green, changing with emotion, maybe. Every time I looked into them, though, they reminded me of the mystery and chaos lurking inside her.

I bit my lower lip and inhaled a deep breath to clear my jumbled thoughts. I slid into the truck beside her and closed the door. The truck was filled with her honey scent and the faint bitterness of copper—the blood that marked us both.

Turning the key, I started the Ford and punched the gas with no idea where to go. We just needed to get away for now; I could figure out our destination when we were miles away.

I was fairly sure Laskin wasn't responsible for sending the Brother I murdered, but he would know about it soon enough. My bet was on Dultsev and his crew, but why didn't they tell Laskin and the bosses? They weren't supposed to make any moves without notifying the Dominion, especially if it was outside their territory. Laskin had briefed me on the Brothers in the area, and Dultsev was not part of this region.

What the fuck is going on here? What did I get myself into?

I just needed to keep my head down from now on and get the job done. Then I could go back home and live out my days protecting my parents in peace.

One sideways glance reminded me there was more at stake, though.

What if I couldn't go through with it?

What if I didn't want to?

Chapter Ten

"Where did you get this truck?" I asked, breaking the silence between Dean and me. We'd bobbed up and down old dirt roads for about an hour, exchanging little more than a suggestion of which direction to go.

"It's one of my mate's," he responded. His fingers clenched the broad steering wheel.

I stared down at a speck of browning blood on my skirt and scraped at it thoughtlessly with my fingernail. Visions of Stuart's last moments danced through my mind, teasing me. He was supposed to be *my* kill. He was supposed to satisfy this unquenchable thirst Dean aroused in my soul.

Stuart's predictable nature ensnared him in my trap, yet, for the first time in my life, I was not the villain who let the black curtain fall over my lover's life.

The more I dwelled on the opportunity I'd lost, the more anxious I became. My body was riling with emotions of lust, betrayal, and anger. Every time I glanced over at Dean from the passenger seat, however, the strange possibilities of "what if" rolled through my thoughts.

What if I didn't have to kill Dean?

What if I could learn to tame this fire burning me from the core?

What if I told him to truth about my past? Would he accept me or turn me in like the serial murderer I was?

He'd killed to protect me. I'd taken lives for the sole purpose of finding a moment's peace in my chaotic heart.

I squinted out into the pitch-black night, searching for familiar landmarks, but it was useless. It seemed like we were heading back to my place at first then he took a left and a right, veering us away from the Charleston peninsula. Outside the city limits, there was an abundance of dark marshes and plantation fields peppered with houses sheltering sleeping families.

If it were daylight, I could figure out exactly where we were. At four o'clock in the morning, I was more lost than a tourist visiting the low country for the first time.

Huffing an exasperated breath, I twisted in the seat and faced Dean. Shadows fanned across his hardened face between streaks of moonlight that filtered through tall oaks lining the road.

"Where are you taking me?" I stared at him, waiting for an answer.

He shook his head once then mumbled something to himself. His hands wrung the wheel as he continued carrying on a conversation without me.

I pursed my lips, annoyed at him ignoring me. "Dean," I yelled, determined to get his attention.

He stomped on the brakes and yanked the wheel to the right, hurling us onto an over-grown, rocky path off the road. Seizing the shifter like he was considering tearing it from the steering column, he slammed the truck into park then threw open his door and hopped out.

Dean marched down the path illuminated by the cloudy headlights for a moment then stopped and raked his hands through his hair. His head tilted up to the star speckled sky.

I opened my creaky door and slid off the seat. Crossing my arms, I moved toward him with the caution of someone approaching a landmine.

"I don't know what I'm doing," he grated, still looking up at the stars.

I couldn't tell if he was speaking to me or to himself again. "Dean?" Unable to see his face or get a definite read on his demeanor, I scrutinized every tick, twitch, and bunch of his muscles. I lifted one hand out to touch his tense shoulder while my other hand guarded the whirling emotions in my middle.

He turned around just as my fingers crested his arm and peered into my eyes. Despite the dark, desperation and confusion was clear in his gray depths.

I fixated on the storm of feelings radiating off Dean and wondered why he was so torn up over Stuart. My intentions were far worse than his, and, as far as he knew, Stuart was going to hurt me. It was defense.

Suddenly, he was on me like the dewy air dampening my skin. He crushed my lips with his, shoving his tongue into my mouth and taking every bit of breath I managed to exhale with my moans. His hands clutched the back of my head, trapping me to him.

This was it…the passion and demanding craze I felt deep inside. He was mimicking the explosive desire raging in my center.

My hands clawed up his hard chest and neck, skimming over the closely shaved hair above his nape. The stubble tickled my fingertips until I plunged my hands into the longer, unruly strands he usually slicked back on the top of his head. I fisted and pulled, coaxing throaty groans from him between ravenous kisses.

With a handful of hair in my grasp, I forced his mouth away from mine. His eyelids snapped open questioningly. We panted, our lips swollen and damp. I stretched up and licked his bottom lip with a slow, teasing stroke of my tongue, still holding his head back. I smirked.

Over the years, I'd learned to read what a man likes and dislikes in the bedroom, and Dean liked to be toyed with, whether he wanted to admit it or not. I lifted onto my tiptoes, resting the back of my upper arms on his shoulders, and caught his lower lip in my teeth. He snarled, but didn't protest. I tugged gently then let it slip from my teeth, observing the lust flaring to a new level in his eyes.

My toes left the ground as he gripped my thighs, hiking my legs up to encircle his hips. I locked my ankles around his waist. His hands slid under my skirt, clawing along the backs of my legs and along the fleshy curve of my ass. He attacked my lips again, invading my mouth and my soul. It was like our tongues fought to get deeper into one another, and I welcomed the brawl.

The world seemed to spin around us, adding to the dizzying swirl of lust entwining between us. Dean began walking, stumbling here and there toward his destination. Beads of sweat and moisture from the humid air gathered on my collar bone, dipping sharply into the divot at the base of my neck. A shiver rolled through my body when the tiny wet bead slithered down my breast bone and disappeared into my heaving cleavage.

Dean leaned down, dipping me backward until my bottom settled onto a cold metal surface. He straightened between my legs and leaned against the truck, trapping me on the wide wheel well beneath me. Spreading my knees farther apart, I let one leg hang over the back of the driver's side tire while the other draped across the headlight, eclipsing the beam that shined on the weed-ridden trail we'd taken. Resting back into the rounded edge of the truck's hood, I gave him a smug look, daring him to succumb to the dirty craving in his eyes.

His shoulders rose and fell around deep, heavy breaths as he studied my face intently for a moment then allowed his gaze to travel down my body. He did it so slowly, and with such yearning, that my core constricted from want. The simple act of him examining me with the same desire I felt made me so wet.

I lowered my hands to my thighs and bunched the blood-stained hem of my dress in my fists. Watching every twitch of his face, each rise of his thickly muscled chest, and every beat of the racing pulse in his neck, I inched the fabric up.

Dean's throat worked around a gulp.

Once I gathered my skirt up enough to reveal the damp spot on my panties, I waited for him to make a move. My hunger for Dean was screaming at me to take control, get what I needed to be sexually satisfied, and then take what I had to have to be emotionally sated. It was a game, though. I'd played it for many years and learned to keep the impulse at bay long enough to drag out the cat and mouse chase. Success was so much sweeter that way.

Dean's large palms spread over the tops of my legs, his fingers sinking into the bend at my hips. He pushed down, pinning me against the wheel well, and bent forward to press a light kiss on my lips. "I want you so badly right now."

"So, take me," I purred, grinning like a Cheshire cat.

I reached down, unbuttoned his pants, and lowered the zipper over the stiff ridge of his cock. Slipping my fingers past the waistband of his underwear, I grazed his plump tip, then wrapped my hand around his engorged shaft.

Dean's eyes closed and his head fell back. A shudder racked his body when I started pumping my hand up and down in lazy motions, squeezing when I neared the end.

He slumped forward, as if the pleasure was too great for him to continue standing, and threw out a hand, slapping it on the hood next to my shoulder. His eyes opened, staring up at me from under his furrowed brow.

"I wanna feel you inside me," I whispered.

Dean growled and straightened. He tugged down his pants and underwear enough to free his cock then snagged my panties aside. The warm breeze felt cool against my hot, damp flesh, but it only made me more sensitive.

I was throbbing inside, writhing with an ache that seemed unreachable.

He licked his lips and smiled. The moisture between my thighs glistened in the moonlight, letting him know that I was more than ready.

His steely grip yanked my hips toward him, the metal squeaking when my cheeks slid along the surface. In one swift movement, he lined his cock up with my slick opening and pushed inside. I gasped, while he groaned. He froze in place, inhaling a ragged breath.

I lay back, arching around the side of the hood. Staring up at the stars, I smiled, memorizing every delicious detail of that moment — the musky perfume of swamp and magnolias, the summer wind…how he felt.

He was a perfect fit, just as I thought; thick enough to fill me to the brim, but not so much that I'd hurt in the morning. His length reached the end of my canal, pressing one of my most sensitive spots, yet he wasn't so long that it felt like a sword was piercing my organs.

I wriggled my pelvis, whimpering from the tease of friction that could bring me to a much-needed climax. He slowly pulled out until it was only the ridge of his swollen tip left inside. The velvety texture of his skin gliding against mine sent an electric shock through my body.

I exhaled, feeling like he'd stolen some small piece of heaven from me before I had enough time to taste it properly.

When he dove back inside, ecstasy drugged my senses, clouding any coherent thought I had before. I cried out with pleasure, lifting my head, hoping to see his emotions laid bare on his face. He was magnificent. Tender with the right amount of roughness. Consumed by the same fire lighting my soul. He groaned, grimacing under the weight of experiencing pleasure so thoroughly.

Satisfaction pulled at my parted lips, appreciating his struggle. I was sure he knew, deep down, that I was trouble — that he shouldn't get involved with me — but the sharp edges of his face and the frenzy in his steely eyes proved he'd jumped overboard a moment too soon and hadn't grabbed a life preserver along the way.

The thumping in my ears drowned out the crickets' chirping and deep croaking of low country frogs watching us from the creek beds cloaked by night.

Dean increased his tantalizing pace, settling into a rhythm which was sure to bring us both to our knees in the end. I barely noticed the truck rocking and squeaking as he thrust in and out of me.

His hands scraped up my waist, encircling my soft belly before reaching higher to cup my breasts. He kneaded and massaged, his hand working to grip the large crests in his palm. Rubbing his thumbs over my puckered peaks, he coiled an invisible knot of desire within me even more.

I threw my head back, stretching my torso in a tense arc toward the stars like an offering to the midnight gods. His cock thickened.

Bulging veins rippled into my hypersensitive opening with each stroke. I slickened, sweet moisture dripping in slow, lazy trails down my folds.

Dean's hand slid up my chest and wrapped around my throat. I rasped out a moan. My pleasure heightened from the control he assumed over me. His chest rumbled with a violent growl, and I grinned between bliss-induced pants.

Then the hunger came. My muscles tightened. My pussy flooded with a rush of release, while my senses zoomed in on the craving to enforce pain.

A roar broke free from Dean's lips, and his body shook and spasmed between my thighs. The hot spurt of his own orgasm blended with mine.

Hooking my ankles around his waist, I locked him into place deep in my sex. I curled up to see the shock on his face when I attacked, but his hand clamped down on my windpipe, slamming me back against the truck's hood.

Chapter Eleven

I sputtered through a feeble gasp, wrenching my fingers around his wrist. He didn't budge. He leaned over me, bringing his face into my line of vision.

"Wha...wha...are...you...doin...?" I wheezed.

His forehead wrinkled. His irises darkened, and his mouth twisted into a sneer.

Dean's grip around my throat faltered for a second, allowing me a half breath, before determination overtook his unsure features again.

"I can't, Vivie. I can't let them do it." Tears glistened in his eyes, sparkling under the moonlight. Bringing his free hand past my face, he smoothed over my hair in a gesture so gentle, it was as if he had two people in his body — two halves, warring over whether to love me or kill me. His "gentle" hand combed through my sweat-damp curls then grazed down my temple and across my cheek. He was trembling. The fierce expression on his face softened. Dean's grip loosened just as the edges of my vision clouded.

I sucked a gulp of air past the raw burning in my throat. "Dean..."

There were many situations where I, the hunter, had become the hunted in my dark years, but this was different. I was always sure that I would come out on top. I knew I could find a way to outsmart those men. But this one. He was different. He was doing things to my body, to my mind, to my emotions that no man had ever accomplished before.

He'd killed for me.

Now, he was killing me.

And I didn't know if I wanted to stop him. Would it be so bad to leave this world? My daddy always told me stories of an afterlife, but I dismissed them. I deemed them tall tales made up by a hopeful man and found little in his words that comforted my unsettled soul.

I scratched my nails up his forearms. Thin threads of blood mingled with the sheen of sweat on his skin. His hand squeezed my neck tighter. Dean's kissable lips pulled over his gritted teeth. A mangled sound of internal struggle tore from his mouth.

"Please, please, forgive me, Vivie," he begged, contradicting his fierce commitment to off me.

The black clouds of strangulation crept into my mind again. I dropped one of my hands from his forearm, and clumsily searched for the emerald pin I'd used to secure my hair. I felt the bite of tiny knifed edges skimming across my scalp as I tugged the pin free.

All I saw now was Dean's face surrounded by a halo of charcoal smudges that quickly closed in around him. I would be a goner soon. I mustered up enough strength to thrust my left hand upward.

Dean roared in pain, released my neck to staunch the steady stream of blood gushing from his right shoulder, then stumbled out from between my legs.

I gasped loudly, the rush of humid air soothing my windpipe. An evening breeze glided over my wetness and cooled my hot sex. Despite his intentions to kill me, I felt broken and abandoned without Dean's closeness, without his cock filling me…without him surrounding and overcoming me.

In that moment, I finally allowed my hidden nature to take over.

There wasn't much that could deter my focus from the end pleasure, but, with Dean, there were moments that I only focused on him, on our being together. The voice that constantly screamed in my head, demanding I take a life, remained a distant whisper—like a demon watching from the shadows—until the very end. He had reversed our roles, though. He'd rendered me vulnerable then knocked me on my ass.

Dean groaned, doubling over a few feet away in the beam of the headlights. He yanked my bladed hairpin out of his shoulder.

I'd barely missed his chest. Had I meant to? I could have jabbed the pin into his lungs and twisted. Another inch to the right and I would've been leaning over his corpse right now, reveling in the rush of his death.

A sharp pang bloomed in my chest at the thought; it was buried behind my ribs and burrowed well beyond the chaos of my devious yearnings.

I rolled off the truck in a bent-over slump, coughing and rubbing my neck to alleviate the soreness. There would be bruises in the morning. It wouldn't be the first time I left with remnants of the battle.

Straightening, I calmed my breathing and turned my attention to the man assessing me with weary eyes. He looked as tortured on the outside as I felt on the inside.

We couldn't leave it like this, though. Tonight had changed our paths.

I set into motion, sprinting toward him before he had a chance to react. I jumped, toppling him to the ground. Blunt pain shot up my legs when my kneecaps hit the gravel, but I paid it no mind. He stared up at me with wide eyes. I clamped my knees around his waist, trapping him to the ground beneath me.

Gritting my teeth, I pulled back my right elbow and hurled my fist down. The sound of bone on bone cracked through the air when my knuckles connected with his jaw. He grunted, bringing his left hand up to comfort his chin. Red seeped out of the tear I made.

Kill him. Don't let him hurt you. He'll use and destroy you. Better to destroy him first, the voice whispered into my mind.

I clasped my right hand around Dean's neck, digging my fingers into the thin layer of skin around his Adam's apple. Using my left thumb, I mashed down on his shoulder wound, coaxing forth more red.

A murky tunnel formed in my image of him. My senses were homing in on my target.

He struggled, pushing up on my bare breast-bone. His mouth formed silent words that made no difference to me.

I noticed the warm bulge of flesh rubbing against my cleft as he bucked and shifted his hips to throw me off. Being a larger girl than most made it harder for them to get away. The challenge was thrilling.

Exhilaration consumed my body. The exquisite friction of his cock rocking along my wet folds spurred shocks of desire to branch along my body like thousands of tiny lightning bolts. I moaned. My eyelids grew heavy with lust around the scene of Dean struggling under my domination.

The air wheezed from his clenched throat, his bulky muscles bunched, trying to gather strength to stop me.

I grinded my pelvis in slow back and forth motions, humming uncontrollable sounds of satisfaction. Lost in the feeling of our connection, my grip on Dean loosened. The voice in the back of my mind became more distant. I didn't really want to hurt him, not like I'd hurt the other ones. Part of me yearned to submit to him without question—even if that meant surrendering my life for whatever purpose he had for killing me.

A gasp rushed from my mouth as my back smacked against the cool ground. My sailor assumed power again by flipping me off him so he could roll on top and capture me under his large frame. Positioning himself between my legs, he peered down at me with narrowed eyes, huffing loud breaths in and out.

"I'll not let you snuff me out like the others," he rasped. Drops of his spittle landed on my face when he spoke. "Why, Vivienne? Why must it be like this?" His angry expression relaxed to one of pity and defeat. "Why do you feel the need to whore yourself out to take some poor schmuck's soul?"

The crack of my hand slapping his cheek was deafening. I slapped him two more times before he wrangled my wrists in his hands and restrained them against the dirt. His jaw tightened, undoubtedly feeling the sting I'd left there.

Tears rolled down my temples. I wasn't mad that he called me a whore. I was pained because I didn't know the answer to his question.

Why *did* I do this? Why *did* I use my body to lure men in so I could murder for that moment's worth of bliss? Better yet, how did he know there'd been others?

"I...I don't know," I responded in a stuttered whisper.

His gaze softened when he recognized my anguish. His mouth crashed down on mine, kissing the breath from me. Our lips tangled in a frenzy of passion and pain, laying every emotion we felt into each other.

He moved both of my hands, stretching them taut over my head to secure them with one of his. Dean's free hand threaded through my hair and fumbled to remove the few harmless pins I'd used to help tack up my curls.

His fingers roamed down my neck, pressing into my skin as if searching for something below my surface. He stopped to plump my right breast and lightly pinch my hardened nipple before moving on to curve his palm around my ribcage.

The warmth of his touch burned into my flesh like a brand, creating a memory I'd later seek out for comfort when I was alone.

Moving over the soft swell of my waist and curvy flare of my hips, he tucked his fingers under the band of fabric connecting my dress bodice to the skirt. He checked the beltline while kissing me like he couldn't breathe without me. His fingers moved on to gather bunches of my skirt in random places, gently squeezing the cloth then grabbing a different area until he'd felt every bit of garment I wasn't laying on.

It took a moment to dawn on me, but I soon realized he was searching me for other weapons. I grinned under his lips.

Once he was satisfied I wasn't hiding anything else, he slipped a finger under my garter and stretched the strap away from my skin. I noted the faint tearing sound then felt the bite of the elastic rip loose and snap my thigh.

He'd torn my favorite garter, but I didn't care. His lips tasted like the most dangerous drug and his tongue like Heaven. That was all that mattered to me.

I bowed my body up toward his chest, needing to be closer to him, but he pulled away. He stopped kissing me. Panting, we stared into each other's eyes, regarding one another with curiosity and fear. He and I were too unpredictable to be trusted, but, beyond the darkness of our souls, we hungered for one another.

Fingertips wandered up my inner thigh, slow and steady. My eyelids fluttered closed. My head pressed back against the ground. I shuddered around a moan. "My God," I exclaimed, sucking in a deep breath.

I don't think I'd ever been wound so tight.

This man…he killed for me, he tried to kill me, and now he was changing every rule I had for this game.

He reached the patch of wet satin covering my entrance. He grabbed the crotch and yanked, tearing my panties. "Why do you women wear so many damn clothes?" he growled.

I hooked my legs around the back of his thighs and pulled, but he held strong, grinning at my failed attempt to take control.

His arm moved between us, and suddenly I felt the smooth, thick head of his cock nudging me open. He sunk into me, forcing a guttural scream to escape my throat. Every cell in my body zinged to life again. I hadn't realized how damaged I felt without him in me. When we were joined, my soul soared and my body hummed.

I couldn't add him to my tally of tattooed hearts, no matter what that voice in my head said.

He slid in and out, still holding me captive by the wrists. I arched up, grazing my breasts against his chest. He, finally, lowered onto me completely and surrounded me with his body. His tongue delved into my mouth, stifling my cries of ecstasy.

How could I have ever wanted to harm this man?

The Fall

Dammit, she feels like paradise.

My dick slid into her soaking warmth, feeling as if it were home, as if she was made for me.

The moment I looked down at her, trapped beneath my body, and glimpsed the turmoil hiding in her darkening hazel eyes, I knew I would surrender to her.

I would sacrifice my life to keep from taking hers.

I didn't know why she had this fury eating at her from the inside out, but I'd let it devour me just to be with her.

Pulling out of her until only my head was in, my body tingled with need, begging me to bury myself in her depths. She squeezed her muscles tight around my dick and dug her heels into my thighs, forcing me in again. I grunted and gnashed my teeth, enraptured by the feel of her.

Vivie's love would surely be the death of me, if she didn't kill me in my sleep first.

I pressed her wrists into the ground, determined to eliminate any chance of assault while I was engulfed in her wiles. We glided against each other, creating an overwhelming friction. She was so wet, I could feel her coating my thighs.

My gaze fell to her bouncing tits, mesmerized by the rocking rhythm we had worked into. Sweat glistened on her beautiful skin, accenting every creamy curve.

I lowered onto her slick body and licked a line from her collarbone to the gentle angle of her jaw. She whimpered, but extended her chin away, granting me easier access.

"Mm, I could eat every piece of your mouthwatering body. You taste so good," I whispered in her ear. I grinned, appreciating the hitch in her breath. She was flipped as upside down as I was.

Gravel ground into my knees, but I didn't feel anything beyond her quivering muscles wrapped around me. I guided one of her hands around my neck and let go, trusting that she wouldn't hurt me. Feathering my fingers along her arm then down her side, I dug them into the plush flesh of her right hip and held her squirming pelvis to the dirt. I plunged all the way to her end.

We both cried out in release, our bodies shaking from tremors of soul-shaking pleasure.

CHAPTER TWELVE

We lay in the grass, gazing up at the changing sky. The first glimpse of morning had peeked past the trees soon after Dean brought me to another climax and surrendered to his own intense release.

Shades of nectarine, lilac, and cotton candy blended in giant puffy clouds above us. We'd settled into the silence and remained there for nearly an hour. Neither one of us, I suspected, really wanted to face the reality of our actions, or where our future would lead us.

Dean's words cut through the deep, even breathing that had filled the space around us. "How many have there been?" he murmured.

"How many what have there been?" I asked, playing dumb.

"The men you've killed...how many, Vivie?"

We stayed as still as we could, my head cradled in the crook of his arm, our bodies entwined at the legs. He didn't want to hear the answer any more than I wanted to admit it.

"Twelve."

He chuckled humorlessly. "I would have been lucky number thirteen then?"

I chose not to respond. Hours earlier, all I could think about was having my way with him then bringing him to heel before I claimed his soul. Now, I wasn't sure I could imagine another day without him.

We barely knew each other, but he knew the darkest part of me, and that meant the world.

"We have to leave here."

I nodded against his chest. "I know. Mr. Dultsev will be coming for me."

Dean shifted, propping up on his elbow so he could look down at me. "I don't think you understand. They've been after you for a while."

Pinching my brows together and shaking my head in confusion, I studied his face. "What do you mean?"

His eyes flicked to the exposed peak of my breast. He bit his lip in contemplation while caressing my nipple with the pad of his thumb. He was avoiding the question.

"Dean? What are you saying?"

He returned his gaze to mine, licked his lips then sat up, wincing as he moved his injured shoulder.

"Who is he, Dean?" I asked, sitting up beside him. I tied the halter of my dress in a messy bow behind my neck and waited for his answer.

"He's part of a Russian brotherhood called the Vladychestvo, or the Dominion. They are separated into sectors all over the world. Billy and Mr. Dultsev are part of one of the sectors known as Svyatyye…the Saints."

I thought about what he said for a moment, recalling the red star on Billy's shoulder and then to the star on Dean's chest. "Are you with them too?"

His head jerked toward me. The dark gray of his irises churned with a deep torment. His head nodded reluctantly. "Some time ago, I was."

"But, not now?"

He pulled his legs up and draped his good arm across his knee, tossing rock he'd picked up from a patch of dirt next to him.

I rested my hand on his bicep. "Are you still with them, Dean?"

He shrugged off my hand and lunged up off the ground. His somber gaze landed on me as he held out his hand. "C'mon. We have to find somewhere to hole-up for a while."

My jaw tightened, and my eyes narrowed. I shoved myself up, ignoring his offer to help. "I'll be just fine, thanks," I scoffed, plucking my shoes from the grass and stamping my bare feet toward the truck. "Take me home." I had told him something I'd never admitted to another soul, yet he was keeping secrets of his own.

His hand latched around my elbow, pulling me to a stop. I sneered back at him and yanked my arm free.

"They'll be after us," he said. He pursed his lips and stepped closer as if the invisible ribbon holding us together had been stretched too far by our distance.

There was always that constant pull with him. I could feel the unpleasant tension build with each inch that separated us, but we were dangerous for each other.

"Us? As far as Dultsev knows, I'm the only one involved in Billy's disappearance. And who's to say they'll link Stuart to either of us? I think I'll take my chances. Don't worry, I clean up after myself pretty well." I stomped toward the truck, snatched the door open, climbed in, then slammed the door shut. Refusing to look at him, I stared down at the dash and waited until he slid in beside me.

The truck sputtered to life, and he steered us back to the main roads. We took a few wrong turns, but I kept my silence, allowing him to figure it out on his own.

I was mad as hell, but I wasn't ready to let him go just yet.

An hour later, we cruised by my house a couple of times, only stopping when Dean was satisfied there wasn't anyone around aside from Betty.

Reaching for the door, I paused and said, "It's probably best you stay away from me from now on. Get as far from me as you can." I glanced over my shoulder at him, and felt a pang in my chest when I saw that his eyes were focused forward. He couldn't bring himself to look at me. "I'm poison to every man I'm intimate with. You'll be no different. One way or another, I'd bring you down." I tugged on the handle and left Dean in the truck alone.

Shoe straps dangling from my fingers, I stood at the end of my driveway, toes sinking into the sand. Behind me was the house I shared with my best friend, who was completely ignorant to my true self.

Ahead of me, the man who knew what hid in my depths and still accepted me drove away.

"Viv? Are you okay?" Betty's concerned voice called out from the front door. Her footsteps slapped down the slats of beach wood lining our walkway. "Sweetie, what happened to you last night? I was worried sick."

When Dean disappeared around the next block, I turned and greeted her with a fake smile. Once again, I fell into the lie that was my life, as if pulling on a second skin that was easy to fit into but just a smidge too tight to be comfortable.

"Dean saw me walking home and insisted on driving me, but we ended up talking all night."

Betty clapped her hands together, smiling from ear to ear. "I knew you two would hit it off. Rich is taking me to the street festival when his ship docks on Friday. You game? We can double."

I stepped onto the walkway and edged past her. "I don't think so, Bet. We really don't have much in common."

"Aw, come on, babe," she drawled in disappointment. "From the mussed hair, grass stains on your back, and smudged make-up, I'm betting you guys had at least one thing in common."

I twisted around to roll my eyes at her, but her waggling eyebrows were too funny to deny. I chuckled and shook my head. "You don't know how to give up, do you?"

She jogged toward me, patting my rump when she stopped at my side. "Never," she bellowed. Betty threw an arm over my shoulders and pulled the screen door open. "You can tell me all about it over some of my famous strawberry muffins."

As much as I wanted to, I couldn't possibly tell her what happened between Dean and I the night before. I wasn't sure I knew what transpired myself.

I cleaned myself up and worked on getting the grass stains out of my dress while Betty danced around the kitchen with a Billie Holiday 45 crooning in the background. The ting of spatulas and spoons bouncing off cooking bowls occasionally echoed down the hall as Betty prepared our breakfast.

The restless craving souring the pit of my stomach nearly every day of my life sprang awake the moment I realized Dean would soon be a phantom of my past.

"Vivienne? They're ready!" Betty yelled down the hall. "Ow, shit," she muttered, likely burning herself on a hot pan. She was great in the kitchen, but sometimes I wondered if she wasn't too clumsy to be near anything above room temperature.

I hung my damp dress on a hanger and hooked it over the shower rod. I'd gotten out what traces of my tryst with Dean I could before convening with my best friend at the dinette.

Betty and I talked at the breakfast table for an hour or so. Her focus was captured by the vague, but somewhat true, details I'd given her about my night. Blurring the lines on a dark truth was something I'd become quite skilled at over the years. Veering too far from the truth made it hard to keep up with.

She lapped up every scrap of dirty details I'd thrown her way, but, in the end, I made it clear there wasn't a future for Dean and me.

"Wow," she huffed, slumping back in her chair and crossing her long legs. Her foot bobbed up and down, flapping a periwinkle, fuzz-trimmed slipper caught around her perfectly-painted pink toes. "What an evening. I'm thinking I got the wrong sailor." She was so cute, it was hard not to giggle at her. She'd gathered her hair in a high ponytail and knotted a sky-blue scarf around her head to hold stray golden curls back from her face. Her green eyes narrowed as her heart-shaped lips widened into a smile. "You surprised me. I didn't think you had a trampy bone in your body. You sure this ain't somethin' more than a one-night stand?"

I nodded regretfully and lowered my gaze to the tea cup sitting on the table in front of me. Fiddling with the porcelain handle, I answered, "I'm sure he's on his way outta town by now."

Betty uncrossed her legs and slapped her hands on her thighs. "Welp, I gotta meet up with Penny and go through her atrocious wardrobe. She's got her first singing gig at Molly's tonight since Gene's out sick, and I promised to help her pick something out that didn't make her look like a cow. What are you gonna do with the rest of your day off?"

Watching the crumbles of tea leaves swirl at the bottom of my cup, I shrugged, then took a sip. "Guess I might see what's going on down at the dock. I could stand some time with the ocean. I hear they have a birthday party planned for Mindy Ferguson."

My best friend stood, frowning, and settled a comforting hand on my shoulder. "Alright, babe. Just don't stay out all night like last night, or I'll be sending the boys to get ya." She smirked, knowing that Big John and Henry would gladly leave their guarding posts at Molly's to chase me down. Both hulking men were sweet on me, but both had too much testosterone, and a few too many scars as proof on their faces, to spark my fancy.

I patted her hand. "Don't worry about me, darlin'. I'll fend for myself just fine."

Tonight, *I* was going to do the chasing.

Tonight, *I'd* seek out something to appease the burning in my gut.

Chapter Thirteen

I examined myself in my compact mirror, reapplying the candy-apple lipstick I saved for my bolder nights. Adjusting the tropical-red hibiscus flowers adorning the right side of my hair, I glanced at the reflection of a man eyeing me from three paces behind.

He was smartly dressed in a blue button-up shirt, brown slacks, and a brown tweed coat which he left open. His coffee-hued gaze roamed over my backside from under the brim of a beige fedora.

I snapped my compact shut and dropped it back into my clutch. Smoothing my hands along the cups and tight seems of my plum sheath dress, I gave the impression of straightening the wrinkles that bunched around my curves, but my intent was to draw the stranger in. The heat of his eyes rolled over my body like southern humidity — thick like smog, but slow and sticky like molasses.

My heels clacked against the pier as I turned and sauntered past the interested man. I made sure to make eye contact on my way deeper into the crowd yelling happy birthday. Mindy cackled, distracting most of the party-goers with her excitement. They cheered and danced to a band performing at the end of the pier. I dodged bodies, careful not to lose the man tailing me.

Emerging from the gathering, I wandered into the quiet shadows of the night and found a secluded place to admire the crashing waves.

Two hands settled on either side of my hips, trapping me to the railing. I grinned. It was like baiting a fish. All I had to do was put the right meat on the hook.

"You shouldn't be out here alone," a low, rich voice rumbled in my ear. A hot body nudged against mine, pressing his growing erection into the seam of my ass. "It's dangerous for such a pretty peach like you," he purred.

I wriggled around to face a handsome face. His dark eyes tried hard to hide his ill-intentions, but I knew what I was looking at. I wondered how many women he'd caught in some corner alone and vulnerable. Unfortunately for him, his tally would come to an abrupt stop with me.

"How foolish of me." I pushed my lower lip out into a pout and fiddled with the buttons on his shirt. "You gonna keep me safe, since you're here?"

The corner of his mouth lifted into a smirk. "Of course, peach."

I slid my hands up his chest and locked them around the back of his neck. Closing my eyes, I stretched up and kissed him. It was tame at first, but the hunger grew, sending me into a frenzy of lust and poison. I opened my mouth and licked his lips, urging him to let me in. He smashed me to the banister with his body and ravaged my mouth, his hands never leaving the railing. Moments later, we separated, gasping for air.

His cock dug into my stomach. Desire soaked my thighs. I'd opted to leave my undergarments at home this time. This needed to be quick, and I didn't want layers of unnecessary fabric to get in the way.

A loud whoop sounded from the party, startling us.

"Let's find somewhere quieter," I whispered.

He nodded, letting me push by. I paused and slipped off my pumps, winking over my shoulder. I led him down a cracked set of wooden stairs leading to the shore.

Inhaling the briny air, I relished the rhythmic sound of waves ploughing into the beach and the bite of sand sifting through my black nylons. He tailed me to a spot bordered by six-foot-high dunes and midnight waters ebbing and flowing nearly to our feet.

Looking back at the man, I noticed we'd roamed down the coastline quite a distance. We couldn't hear the band anymore, and the dock lights were no more than tiny stars beaming on a drunken group of lively people. This was far enough.

I dropped my shoes in the sand and crooked my finger at my victim, beckoning him into my web.

"Ah, honey. You're in for it," he promised with a mischievous grin.

His jacket thumped to the ground. He toed off his shoes and tugged off his socks, leaving them in his wake. His fingers made quick work of undoing his belt, pants button, and zipper.

I stood, still dressed, allowing him to walk right into my trap.

He stopped inches from me, winded from the shear thrill of what was going on. I suspected our ideas of what would happen next were very different, though.

I shoved his pants and underwear down then ripped his shirt open, showering the ground with buttons. A challenging growl erupted from his throat. I bit my lower lip and peeked up at him with feigned shyness and shock at my own strength.

He laughed. Leaning down, he kissed me hard, smashing my lips against my teeth. I shoved him to the ground. His eyes widened, stunned that lil' ol' me would take control like that.

Hovering over him, I stood with one foot on either side of his waist. "What was that you said?" I asked, tapping my finger on my lips in contemplation. His lipstick smeared lips opened to answer, but I interrupted. "Oh, that's right, honey. 'You're gonna get it.'"

I grabbed a handful of my straining dress and shimmied it up over my hips. As I lowered, I slipped my fingers under the hem of my stockings and pushed them down to my ankles so my bare thighs mounted his hips like a saddle.

Raking my nails up his defined abdomen and hard pecs, I urged his shirt aside. A small red, six-pointed star marked the base of his neck where his jugular disappeared into his chest. My breath faltered. I hesitated.

He was one of them.

Did he know who I was?

I licked my lips and simpered. I could do this. He wasn't any different than Billy or Stuart. Or Dean. Just another man to die in my arms.

I needed that feeling. I couldn't go another day without a release.

The man bucked his hips, stealing me from my thoughts.

His lips curled up, amused. "Like what ya see, peach?"

I leaned back and nodded, gliding my slick seam back and forth across his shaft.

The man groaned. "Well now, you're as sweet as a kitten. They told me you were gonna be trouble, that I'd have to do you quick," he panted. His hand reached for my breasts and groped them until they felt bruised.

So, he did know who I was. His admission threw me a bit, but I forced myself to continue with my plan. There was no stopping now; we both knew too much.

I continued rocking against him, allowing the sensation of his cock rubbing my bud to bring me closer to climax. "Who told you I was gonna be trouble?" I purred.

He made a clicking sound with his tongue twice, then answered, "Oh, just some friends of mine. I thought I'd have a go at ya, though. I promised them you'd never see me comin'."

The man sat up and wrapped his arms around me, grinding me down on him harder. He tried to wriggle inside me, but I tilted my pelvis, and he missed my entrance.

"Come on, peach. You know you want it." His lips crushed mine, suffocating me in a hard, sloppy kiss.

Unable to break free of him, I reached for my right foot and tugged off my stocking. My hands met behind his neck, and I pulled the nylon tight.

He held me by the back of the head, holding my mouth to his as he twisted and licked crudely. I bowed my back away from him and squeezed my hands between us where I crisscrossed the ends of my stocking.

I grunted and mumbled into his mouth, trying to tell him to stop, to let me go, but he only gripped me harder.

Finally, I sunk my teeth into his bottom lip. When he jerked back, I yanked my hands apart, snapping my stockings into a tight band around his neck.

He let go of me and pried at the taut fabric cutting into his throat. I wound my wrists in fast circles, wrapping the nylon around my hands for better control. Thrusting my arms out, I forced the man backward, his spine slamming into the soft sand.

He opened his mouth, gasping for air, struggling to rasp out some bullshit words I wasn't interested in. His fingers clawed at my chest and neck, eager to get a hold on me and assume power. I scooched my body forward and restrained his arms under my knees, trapping them to the ground by the biceps.

Leaning down until our noses touched, I stared at his glossy eyes and said, "You clearly underestimated me, honey. I'm a fucking tigress,

126

not a kitten." I gritted my teeth and laid all my weight into pressing down on his arms and wrenching the stocking.

The man's fight left him within seconds. I observed, soaking up the sight of veins lining his forehead, neck, and temples plumping into thick ropes. His skin flushed to a deep reddish-purple, and strings of spit clung to his lips and teeth as he tried to mouth "Stop."

Hunger for this moment coiled in my belly, riveting all my senses, waiting for that sweet release.

His hands flopped to the sand, creating tiny, beige clouds that puffed into the air then swirled away on the ocean breeze. A soft pop resonated from his throat where I'd likely broken the small bone that curved around his windpipe. His jaw laxed, his eyes glazed over, and his chest stilled.

I moaned at the glorious exhilaration flooding my body. The automatic response always left me feeling like a lover had touched me just right—dampening my sex, beading my nipples, and puckering my skin. The rush of adrenaline flew me higher than the clouds.

But, as usual, the high always came with a low.

Chapter Fourteen

"It's okay, devushka. You just take da knife an' cut right here," the man with the funny voice instructed as he dragged his finger across the tied-up person's neck. His words were kinda like Mommy's but much funnier.

Whimpers sounded from under the black hood. The mister tied to the chair was breathing fast. I could tell because the front of the hood kept blowing up like a balloon, and then falling like someone had poked it with a needle. I giggled at how it was blown up, then not blown up, blown up, then not blown up.

"Pay attention, you little beetch," the man with the funny voice — Boris, I think my mommy called him — yelled at me. I stopped giggling. He meant business. He called my mommy that word, beetch, a lot, and it was always right before he gave her a bad spanking and made her cry.

I stared up at the mister in the chair and tightened my small, chubby fingers around the sharp knife's handle just like Boris taught me.

"Dat's it, devushka," Boris praised. "Come on, girl, we don' have all day."

I shuffled my feet forward, pleased with the clack of my new pretty shoes Boris had given me as a present earlier. They sounded like Mommy's shoes. I was just like Mommy. I'd watched her use the same knife many times before. I could do it too.

Tugging on the mister-in-the-hood's pants, I crawled onto his lap and stood with one pretty shoe on each of his legs. Hot air blew through the hood. I scrunched my nose at the bad breath puffing in my face.

"Vivienne," my mommy squeaked in a trembling voice.

I glanced over at her and noticed her cheeks were wet. Her eyes looked so sad. They jumped from me to the mister, then to Boris.

"Please," she said quietly, shaking her head at the man with the funny voice. "I'll do it. Please, just let her go." Her fingers pressed together like when she prayed, then she clasped them over her lips.

I peeked up at Boris, confused about why Mommy was crying, but his eyes were on her, not me. He nodded his head, without looking at me. "Now, devushka, before I lose my patience."

Resting my free hand on the mister's chest, I reached the knife forward and moved it in the same motion Boris had instructed. The black hood split open, and a thin red line appeared on the mister's throat, playing peek-a-boo. He hissed and jerked, knocking me off balance. I fell to the floor and began crying. My butt hurt from landing so hard, and I was scared.

Mommy was screaming now, but when she moved to help me up, the big, scary man behind her grabbed her arms and held her in place.

"Kukla," Mommy cried her special name for me. "You're okay, baby doll. Just get up." She nodded at me, calming my fear from afar.

"Get up and finish, little beetch. I didn't give you those shoes for nothing," Boris snarled.

"I...I don't wanna," I hiccupped between sobs.

Boris stomped toward me, yanked me off the ground by my arm, then picked up the knife and shoved it in my hand. I cried harder, now, because my arm hurt. He was being so mean.

"You will do what I say," he spat. His rough hand lifted me up into the air, carrying me like I carried my dollies.

Mommy yelled at Boris, using the same funny words he used sometimes, from her spot by the wall. The big man clapped his hand over her mouth.

Boris propped me onto the mister's lap again and jerked my hand holding the blade up. "Deeper this time, or I will hurt your dear mommy. Ponimayu?" He paused, glaring at me with meanness in his eyes. "Understand?"

I nodded and sniffled. Leaning into the mister's chest, I put both hands on the knife's handle and dug it into his neck, dragging it from one side to the other.

Red sprayed out at me, messing up my dress. Mommy will be so mad at me.

"Goot girl," Boris bellowed behind me, letting out a laugh that filled the room. "Goot girl." He pulled the knife from my hand and helped me off the mister, who was quiet now.

I'd made him all better. He wasn't scared anymore.

"Anton," Boris called, "take her to da clients. We'll start the second lesson today."

Anton rushed to my side and swooped me up in his arms. His eyes were wet. "Come, little one. Let's get you cleaned up. They don't like messy little

131

girls to play with. How about a pretty new dress to match your new shoes?"
He smiled.

I nodded, letting him carry me to my next lesson. I liked Anton; he was kind. Wrapping my arms around Anton's neck, I laid my head on his shoulder. My eyes landed on Mommy.

She reached an arm out for me, as if she could touch me from all the way across the room, while she struggled to get away from the big man.

Cackling echoed along the shore, drawing me back from a bad daydream and reminding me of the people not too far away.

I unwound my fingers from the ruined strand of nylon, ignoring the red indentions striping my hands, and let it fall on the ground. It spread out on either side of his bruising neck like a scarf blowing in the wind.

Sitting upright, I looked to the stars, swallowing hard and huffing from utter exhaustion.

Flattening my hands on his chest, I pushed myself to my feet. My legs felt like wet noodles. I stepped to his side and shoved my dress down, glowering at his vacant gaze. He seemed so harmless from here.

He was going to kill you, I assured myself. *You had to kill him.*

I knew better. I lured him into my clutches without a second thought as to whether I'd let him live or not. It had always been that way. I only felt the remorse creep in after the deed was done.

Bending over, I yanked the stocking from around his neck then stumbled to the side and fell to my knees. With all fours digging into the sand, I threw up every bit of the liquor and hors d'oeuvres I'd ingested earlier. My shoulders shuddered around a sob of confusion.

Why did I have to do this? Why couldn't I just live a life of normalcy, instead of having to hide this terrible secret?

I jerked when a screaming whistle resonated from the distance, followed by a thunderous boom. The sky crackled. A bright shower of white lights cast a glow over the crime scene I'd just created. I swallowed the sour saliva flooding my mouth and wiped the remnants of puke from my chin with my stocking.

I shuffled handfuls of sand over my vomit, then crawled to my shoes. Gathering my belongings, I stood and scanned over his body one last time, making sure I'd left nothing behind.

Turning to head farther down the beach, where no one from the party would spot me, I veered to the right on unsteady feet and toppled into a sand dune. My thoughts whirled around in my head like a tornado, then I fell into a deep, consuming sleep.

THE WITNESSING

Looking down from a mound of sand, I saw everything.

From the second he found her in the crowd and marked her as his target, the stranger in the fedora watched her like prey.

When she started showing an interest in him, thinking he was just some gent following her, I fisted my hands at my sides, restraining my rage, and decided to let it all play out. I wandered in the background, keeping a distance so she wouldn't notice me, but I tracked their every move.

I had to see if it was true, so I let it happen, and now I knew.

She was a murderer.

I wasn't angry that she killed him, though. I knew he was a low-life womanizer who'd worked his way up the Dominion ranks. He was one of the area Brothers Laskins had pointed out. I was angry that he had her attention, that she was rubbing herself all over him. I should be the only one between her legs, and I should be the only one giving her what she needed.

My heart ached at the realization that I might never be able to give her what she desired. If she had some deep-seated need to kill, I would never be able to satiate Vivienne.

The flush in her cheeks, the lust in her troubled eyes, and the sense of control behind her movements indicated she'd done this many times before. This was her nature. It was like breathing to her. And, God help me, I couldn't seem to care enough to walk away.

Now, she lay in a quiet heap in the sand. If someone found her, she'd be arrested. Maybe, that's what she needed.

I wasn't going to let that happen though.

Damn her for dragging me into this. This was twice that blood shed over her stained my hands too.

Damn her for making me love her.

Chapter Fifteen

I woke to an orange ray of setting sun shining across my eyes like a spotlight in an otherwise dark room. I threw my arm over my face, shielding against the horrid glare.

"You're up," a gruff voice said from a shadowy corner.

I sat up, squinting into the darkness. The silhouette of a large figure sat in a chair positioned in the blackest part of the room.

"Dean?" I asked wearily.

He leaned forward, the angles of his face highlighted by the edge of sun beam.

"I thought you'd left."

His hands scrubbed down his tired expression. Days-old stubble was fast turning into a black beard. Blue circles were forming under his stormy eyes.

"I did, but then…I didn't." Standing from the chair, he started pacing back and forth at the foot of the bed I was on.

I took in the small room containing the bed, an olive-hued tufted chair, and a small nightstand. We were in a hotel room.

"Where are we?"

He didn't answer.

I scooted to the side of the mattress and swung my legs over the edge, noticing I only had one stocking on. Panic swelled in my chest. "My stocking. Where is my other stocking?"

Dean stopped and turned toward me. He stuffed his hand into his pant pocket and pulled a thin, black ribbon of fabric back out with it.

I closed my eyes and exhaled. "Oh, thank God."

"Why?" he whispered.

My lids snapped open. If he took me from the beach, he probably knew why the stocking was so important, but maybe he needed me to admit it.

"Because it's evidence," I confessed. Shame pressed down on me like a ton of bricks.

"No," he shouted. He balled up the stocking and threw it at me then began pacing again. "Why did you kill him? Why did you kill any of them?" His fingers threaded through his unkempt hair.

"I don't know. It's just...," I lowered my gaze to my hands, wringing the stretched nylon. "It's just something I need to do. I dream about it—since I was a little girl, really—and this urge, it's constantly lingering in the back of my mind. I can't get past it. I've tried."

Dean moved to the window, staring out at the hotel lot. He couldn't even bear to look at me anymore. "When was the first one?"

"I'm not sure, but I think when I was sixteen."

When my hormones kicked into overdrive, the impulses to hurt the boys I was with exploded. I told myself they were accidents at first, but I knew better.

"You're not sure?" he shouted.

I startled from the booming anger in his voice. "No," I whispered. "There's times I can't decipher between dreams and reality. I feel like this started much earlier, but..." I shrugged one shoulder and wrapped the stocking around my palm, silently enjoying how the restriction reminded me of my last kill. Berating myself, I continued, "It's as if I've lived two people's lives—one when I was little, and the one I live now." I shook my head, realizing how crazy I sounded.

"These flashbacks play in my mind after my kills—terrible things from when I was a child—but they can't be real. My parents wouldn't have let me do those wicked things."

My gaze darted to his back, pleading for some absolution he couldn't give me. "Right? Parents don't let their little girls murder people or have sex with grown men, right?" Tears stung my eyes.

He turned. His brow furrowed in an expression of disbelief and pity.

"Dean?" I cried. "I need help. I don't wanna be this monster, but I can't stop."

My bones rattled from the sobs pouring out of me. I'd wound the stocking so tight around my fingers that they were going numb, but the discomfort helped me stay grounded.

Dean stalked to my side and sat on the bed next to me. He folded me in his arms while I wept.

139

He was the only one I'd ever told. It felt so good to finally get it off my chest, yet it solidified how damaged I was. Before I admitted it out loud, I could pretend the murders were just a figment of my imagination.

"I don't know how to help you, Vivie. I'm not sure you understand the grave situation we're in."

I pulled out of his embrace and scoffed, "And, you do?"

His lips pursed, holding back the frustration lining his face. "I have a theory, yes."

"Let's hear it then." I sniffled, wiping my tears away with the back of my hand.

Silence filled the room while he considered how to approach the subject properly. He rubbed his hands down his face again, rolling ideas around in his mind, clearly trying to decide what to tell me and what to keep hidden.

"Out with it, Dean," I demanded.

"Dammit, woman," he snapped, "give me a minute."

I rose off the bed and traced his steps, back and forth, at the bed's end. The orange streak of sunlight slashing across the floor was slowly creeping out of the room. Dusk was coming. I must've been out for a while. It seemed the physical and emotional upheaval of the last few days was taking its toll on me.

"I was supposed to kill you."

His low, gravelly voice stopped me in my tracks. My head jerked toward him. "What?"

It was almost comical. All this time, *I'd* done the killing. Sure, I knew he meant to kill me the other night, but hearing him say it — that he was "supposed" to do it — like it was a job, was a little jarring. I crossed my arms over my midsection, suddenly feeling very exposed.

"I didn't have a choice." He shook his head. "No, that's a lie. I did have a choice...I chose you." His sullen eyes landed on me. He clasped his hands together between his knees as if he were praying.

"As opposed to what?" I whispered.

"My parents."

My gaze dropped to the last remnants of sunlight coloring the dull, fern pattern on the carpet. Shame pierced my heart. I never asked him to choose me. I didn't deserve it, especially not over his family.

"Were you hired to kill me because of Billy?"

Dean shook his head. "I think, because of them all."

"What do you mean, 'because of them all'?" I squeaked.

"I mean, Billy was under the Saints. It was one of the higher-ups with the Demons — the Demony — who approached me. He told me you had killed many of his men. He and Mr. Dultsev control different sectors of the Dominion. Both gangs have lost brothers to you."

"But, I only saw the tattoos on Billy, Stuart, and maybe one oth...," I let my words trail off in thought. Were they the only ones? I didn't see *all* my victims naked.

"Vivie, I have a hunch there were more than you realize."

Dean lunged off the bed and rushed to me. His hands settled on my shoulders in a gesture of comfort. He ducked down, pulling my attention to his gray eyes. "He said you were an experiment gone wrong. You don't remember being a part of the Dominion?"

I inched my head to the right about to shake it then stopped and tilted it to the side. Did I remember being involved with a gang? The memories of killing a man as a child echoed against my skull. What about the memories that I didn't acknowledge, the ones scratching right below my surface, only coming out in dreams or flashbacks? Those were mostly when I was a child too. Were they reality? Had I been a killer even then?

I plunged my hands into my hair and squeezed my head, trying to recall the images I had long ago buried with my mother. "I...I don't know. There may have been more."

"Think, Vivie. From what I've pieced together, they made you this...," his sentence died, unfinished.

"This what, Dean? This monster?" I spat. "They made me the monster I am today?" Sobs broke free from my chest. My body quaked from the anger and despair ravaging my insides. "Why would they do this?" I pounded my fists against his chests as he tried to pull me into his arms. "Why didn't you just kill me?"

Dean circled his arms around me and held me tight, whispering kind words of consolation.

I could have been someone different. I could have been normal. I might not have been born with this evil urge inside me after all. No matter now, though. The bodies have piled up, and the backlash was catching up to me fast.

"How many do you think were gangsters?" I asked, once I calmed. His shoulders shrug against me.

"I don't know. Maybe all of them. At least three: Billy, Stuart, and Gregory."

I leaned back to look at him. "Gregory?"

"He was the man on the beach. I found his wallet." He nudged his chin toward a small, dark lump on the nightstand.

"It can't be possible that *all* the men I've been with and killed were part of this elaborate scheme to capture me for the Dominion…can it?"

What if they *all* were criminals sent to trap me or kill me? That meant my entire life had been planned—forced in a way. It meant I'd been manipulated with every sexual encounter I'd had. Would I receive some reprieve for that? Because they weren't innocent men? In my heart, I knew it was unlikely. These were sins I would carry beyond my grave. Even if they were the worst men on Earth, it didn't wipe away any of the devious things I'd done to satisfy my hunger.

"Anything is possible with these men, Vivienne. They have power like nothing you've seen before. They have hidden connections and money everywhere."

I wriggled out of his arms and began pacing the room again. How would I get out of this? I thought I'd been careful all this time, but if they were all Brothers, every one of them knew I was coming. Hell, they'd planned on it. Their attempts just failed. If that was the case, then this Dominion knew too much about me. I couldn't turn them into the Police; it would implicate me too.

Stopping in front of the window, I watched the neon lights of the Oasis Inn sign flicker on. "We have to kill them," I exhaled.

He laughed, then stopped when I turned and looked at him with a straight face.

"Vivie, we can't kill them. Trust me, if it could be done, I would have long ago. There's too many, and we have no way of knowing who they all are. Hell, most of them aren't even in the States, but there's enough to be a problem for us both."

"What do you suggest then, Dean? If what you say is true, they will find me no matter what. Maybe not today or tomorrow, but they will find me, no doubt. Now you're in danger, too."

He closed the distance between us, engulfing me in his warmth. "Oh, darling. I've never been out of danger, if I'm honest with myself. I was born into the Dominion and when I came of age, I vowed to take my papa and mama far away from them. My papa had a hit out on him because he refused to beat a local butcher for missing a rent payment. The Demons' boss owns most of the small town we lived in. We fled, and the butcher was beat to death the next day." He blew out a guilt laden breath.

"We are considered traitors now. I've been hiding them here in the states, but they found us anyway. I figured, they learned I was a trained sailor and thought I'd have a better chance than some of their minions. I was given the choice to kill you or my parents would die."

I stepped into him, caressing my hand over his stubbled check. "Why would you choose me? What about your family?"

Lowering his head, he kissed me, long and slow. "Let me worry about them," he breathed against my lips.

As our mouths explored each other's, he guided me toward the bed. The edge of the mattress pressed into the back of my knees. Dean hooked his arm around my waist and lifted me up, tossing me on the plush surface.

A sly grin formed on his mouth. He unbuttoned his shirt one by one, his steely eyes drinking me in from head to toe. He unbuckled his belt and opened his fly. "I've been waiting to do this since I saw you with that loser on the beach."

Leaning over, he snagged the hem of my dress with his thumbs and shoved it up until he could see my bare sex. He bent one knee and rested it onto the bed, then the other, positioning himself between my legs. His fingertips skimmed along my skin, starting at my ankle and ending at the top of my thigh.

I gasped, rolling my pelvis to urge his hand to continue.

His eyes fixated on my wet folds, and he hummed a sound of satisfaction. Two fingers slid into my opening. I arched my back up and cried out. He started a slow advance and retreat, rubbing on just the right spot to make me cream.

My breaths grew faster, my eyelids heavy with lust.

Dean used his other hand to slip the remaining stocking off my leg while he continued playing me. Suddenly, I was empty, and he was bending over me to grab one of my hands. He bound the nylon around one wrist, looped it around a slat of the headboard, then tied the free end around my other wrist.

I shuddered and gazed up at him, feeling more vulnerable than I ever have. At the same time, I experienced a sense of freedom that had always eluded me.

He gripped my left ankle, stretching it up in front of him, then crossed it over to lay on top of my right ankle. His hands latched onto my hips and shifted me in one quick motion, so my lower half twisted to rest on my right side.

I stared at him with a heat scourging me so intensely inside, I could've melted before he entered me.

Two of his fingers plunged into my dripping wetness once more, drawing a long moan from my lips. "This is mine, Vivienne. There'll never be another man here. Do you hear me?" His tone was virile, determined.

He was claiming me—and the untamable fire that destroyed everything it touched.

"Do you hear me, Vivienne?" he barked, cracking his hand across my ass-cheek.

"Yes," I exhaled. "No one else." I grunted on an up thrust of his fingers.

There would be no one else, but him, ever again. No other could satisfy my hunger like him.

He groaned, removing his fingers one second and pushing his cock inside my slit the next. The fit was so tight with my legs pressed together, I struggled to catch my breath. The sensation was too much.

He held still with his pelvis flush against my rear, fully seated to my end, waiting for me to adjust. When I found air again, I wiggled, coaxing him to move.

Dean set into a fevered rhythm, slamming against my ass and legs, filling me to the brim with each thrust.

His constant pounding against my most sensitive spot rocketed me to Heaven. My skin writhed like I might detonate at any moment. My belly spasmed. My body singing a song only he could've written.

I screamed out an orgasm, shivering from the explosion. He soon followed, his tip swelling and his back stiffening before he released in my depths.

CHAPTER SIXTEEN

"Daddy? Can you hear me?" I whispered into the receiver.

Sitting on the chilly, tiled floor in the bathroom, I scooted along the wall until my legs were pulled in enough to shut the door most of the way. I dragged the telephone closer, fingering the coiled telephone cord anxiously.

"Dad, are you there?" I spied on the body resting peacefully on the bed through the crack.

"Viv, is that you, baby?" His voice was raspy in that way it got after snoring for a spell. He cleared his throat. "Everything okay, kid? What time is it?" The sound of his hand scrubbing over his beard came through the earpiece.

"It's eleven-fifteen, Daddy. I have to ask you something."

"Anything, baby, but, you couldn't have done this in the morning?" He let out a sleepy chuckle.

"No. I need to know now."

"Okay, okay. I'm listening. Hey, why are you whispering?"

"Never mind that." I rolled my eyes, propping my elbows on my knees, and hiding my face in my palm. "What happened when I was little, Daddy? Before Mom died?"

A moment of silence filled the line between us. "I'm not sure what you're talking about."

"I'm not stupid. I know something happened. Please, just tell me. Please," I begged on the verge of tears.

"Who have you been talking to? Did they find you, Vivienne? Are you with them now?" His questions tumbled out in a nervous rush.

"Who is 'they'?" I bit my upper lip to keep the building cries from escaping. He knew, and he never told me. My own father kept this horrid past from me.

"I thought they'd forgotten about you," he croaked out. He cleared his throat again. "I figured they had accepted your mom's sacrifice and moved on."

Flashbacks of that night—the freezing, surging waters and angry storm—appeared in my mind. The pale glow of moonlight illuminating her face as she sunk deeper below the surface. "Be careful who you trust, they have eyes everywhere," she'd said.

My mother had killed herself to protect me?

"Dad, who are these people, what did they do to me?"

He sighed into the receiver. "I only know the stories your mother told me. She was so afraid when she found me.

"I was living in Italy. I did the fisherman thing for a while after I left the military. You mother came running up to me with this frightened little girl one day, begging me for help. She was so beautiful, and you were…so young and innocent. That day, I gave her my heart. I gave you both my heart." He paused. "You don't remember any of this?"

I felt like the floor had dropped out beneath me, like all the air was sucked out of the room. The vague familiarity of that day played in my mind.

I did remember.

Why did it take him reminding me? How many of my memories were buried so deep that I'd forgotten entire pieces of my life? Did I want to remember?

"Viv? You there?"

I wiped away a tear trickling down my cheek. "Yeah, Dad, I'm here." I had decided, that day, the nice fisherman would be my new father. Until now, I had forgotten there was a time that he wasn't. "What did mama say she was running from?"

"Well, she said she was the daughter of a Russian gang member. She was forced to live a life of crime and undermining government groups. Irena wouldn't tell me the details, but I always got the feeling, it was hell for her…and you.

"I agreed to hide y'all in a small shack I was renting. She never told me how she managed to get out of Russia with you, but I'm willing to bet she had some inside help."

The scraping sound of dry feet shuffling along a wood floor traveled up the line. I pictured him in the kitchen, brewing coffee.

"Those were the best months of my life. Though Irina didn't talk much about the past, we found love in the present. I was kind to her, and in return, she gave me a family.

"I got a job offer back here in the states, and she insisted I take it. A few days before we were scheduled to leave, we took my old Schooner out and…well, you know the rest." His voice became grief-laden. "She'd met with someone the day before we boarded. Said it was a friend she'd met at the market, but I wonder now if it wasn't someone from her past. I think they may have warned her, and that was why she…why she jumped."

Liquid poured into a cup on the other end. "I think they were looking for you. She mentioned that they might come for you. Never said who 'they' were specifically. She made me promise I'd take care of you if anything ever happened to her." He slurped on something. "That's what I did, kiddo. I took care of you. Best I could anyway."

"Yeah, you did, Daddy," I assured him.

He slurped again. "I'm a little surprised you don't remember any of that stuff." He blew his nose, likely into one of his many dingy handkerchiefs he tucked in his pocket every morning. "Ah well. It's for the best, I suppose. Your little mind was probably too fragile for whatever you saw those fools do."

I *had* remembered some of it, though. The past had leaked through cracks in my wall as I got older, bleeding through just enough for me to know I had no innocence as a child, and I would have none as an adult.

Images of Boris encouraging me to slit the hooded man's neck flashed in my mind. Bile stuck in my throat. I was disgusted with the woman they'd made me.

"Thanks. I'll call again soon," I whispered with a trembling bottom lip.

"Hey, Vivienne...tell me what's going on...please."

I shook my head. "Nothing you need to worry about, Daddy. I'll talk to you soon. Love you." Setting the phone back on the base, I let the tears flow. I wept into my hands as quietly as I could, so I wouldn't wake up Dean.

Once I got my crying under control, I picked up the telephone, turned off the bathroom light, then crept back to the bed. I set the base down without making a noise, but I couldn't bring myself to crawl back in bed with this man.

He'd taken such a risk by not killing me. I couldn't let his family suffer for me.

His beautiful body sprawled over most of the mattress, a sheet covering his lower half, except for his left foot.

It would be so easy to give in. All I'd have to do is hit him with the lamp on the nightstand. Just keep beating him until he didn't wake up ever again.

I drew in a deep breath and squeezed my eyes shut, willing the thoughts away. The urge quieted after a few seconds. I picked my dress up off the floor and shimmied into it without looking at Dean. I grabbed my shoes and eased the door open.

Hesitating, I kept my gaze on the parking lot, but all I could see in my mind was Dean's face looking at me with love in his eyes.

I stepped over the threshold.

The Disappearance

"Vivienne," I croaked, blinking my eyes to adjust to the neon-green light seeping through the inch of space between the curtains. I coughed and cleared the frog from my throat. "Vivienne, you up, babe?" Patting the cold spot next to me, I realized she was not in the bed with me. The room was dead silent. I sat up and rubbed the sleep from my eyes.

I unraveled the sheet around my waist and rose from the bed, noting the bathroom door was open and the light was off. Vivienne's stockings were strewn across the floor, but her dress and shoes were missing. I raked my hands through my hair and spun, searching the room for hints that she planned to return. My gaze landed on the sliver of light shining into the room from the slightly cracked door.

"Fuuuck," I yelled. Where could she have gone? "Settle down, Dean. Maybe, she went out to get us breakfast." I glanced at the small

155

clock ticking next to the bed. It was three in the morning. Seemed plausible, but my gut was screaming that they took her. Every bone in my body was vibrating with the fear that Laskin's men tracked us down and stole her in the night. Logic told me otherwise. If they came to take her, they would have, surely, shot me in my sleep. They had an ideal opportunity.

I grabbed my pants off the chair, hopping into them one leg at a time, then snatched Vivienne's stockings off the faded carpet and stuffed them in my pocket. Shoving my feet into my shoes, I slung on my shirt. After one more sweep of the room, I hooked a finger in my keyring, snagging them off the dresser as I headed out of the hotel room.

They were not gonna win if I could help it.

I didn't care what she'd done in the past; I was gonna change Vivienne's future if it took my last breath.

Chapter Seventeen

I hurried over the uneven streets of downtown Charleston. A prim-looking woman threw me a side glance as she hugged her date's arm tighter and passed by me with quickening steps. Her beau grinned, letting his eyes linger on my curves longer than appropriate.

My hair lay in messy curls over my right shoulder, tamed only by my ruby, rose hairpins, as opposed to neat coifs most ladies wore in public. My fitted black capris and button-up blouse said I was a woman up to no good. I was a gal with a plan.

I'd had little time to waste when I went home to shower and change. Why bother with taming my hair and applying rouge? Hell, I barely cared enough to button my blouse to the third button. I didn't know what would be in store for me later, and I wanted to be comfortable.

Thank God, Betty was gone and couldn't talk me out of it. She might've tied me down to a chair just to get me to stay.

As I approached Molly's, there was only one thing on my mind — finding Mr. Dultsev. If anyone could get me close to the Dominion bosses, I had a feeling it was him. He'd been quite the regular at Frankie's bar over the last week, so I was confident I'd find him there tonight.

I skipped down the steps and banged on the door. "Frankie, it's me. Let me in," I shouted, pounding again.

A muffled voice permeated through. "I'm comin', I'm comin'. Hold your goddamn horses."

Seconds later, Frankie greeted me, holding the door open with an irritated expression. "Come on in, princess," he mocked in an extra sweet tone.

I shoved past his protruding belly, pausing to kiss his cheek as usual, then continued into the dim underground club. My eyes adjusted quickly, used to the atmosphere from endless nights working there. The ground thumped with the beat of Jim's drumming while Gene squalled out a tune on stage.

My gaze surveyed the sparse crowd, looking for my target. The evening was ending, so most late-night partyers had gone home. It didn't take long for my ears to register Vera's signature cackling from across the room. Next to her, I found the short, round man I was looking for.

I straightened, resolve strengthening my confidence, and made a beeline for their table. Luckily, there wasn't a large group around him to witness the scene I might cause.

Mr. Dultsev's body jiggled around a deep, husky laugh as if someone at his table told a joke. Vera sat on his lap, chattering with the gal next to her. The picture of the two together was so odd, much like a blonde twig perched on a bullfrog's leg.

I stopped beside the table and cleared my throat. They continued their mindless banter like I was nothing more than a gnat bothering them. Clearing my throat again, I stared right at the ugly Russian and waited for him to look up.

"Yeah, sweetheart, I'll take another one of these here tonics," a skinny man with orange hair and freckles ordered, before smacking me on the ass.

I glared down at him, making my intentions clear that if he tried that shit again, I might break his hand. His laughter died. When I returned my attention to the bulldog of a man to his left, he was staring back at me with a knowing grin.

"Ms. Carson," he tipped his head, finally acknowledging my presence. The motion made his double chin bigger. This man was the epitome of glutton with his stout, pudgy body and high, snooty nose.

I was about to crumble his tall ego under my heel and give him a taste of feeding from the bottom like the rest of us.

Leaning in closer to his oily face, I flattened my hands on the table. "We need to talk."

159

He studied me for a moment, considering my demand. He slapped Vera's behind then nudged her off his knee. She pushed her bottom lip out, pouting, and groaned. He stood, barely meeting my eye-level. "Let's talk, then, devushka," he conceded in his thick accent.

Vera plopped down in Dultsev's chair, shooting darts at me with her eyes for stealing her date's focus.

I spun and led the Russian out of Molly's, ignoring Frankie and Al's concerned expressions. I had business to take care of, but I wouldn't do it at the expense of those I cared about. We'd take this outside.

The hot night air and the angry fire in his eyes caused a sheen of sweat to drip down the back of my neck. I guided Dultsev to a secluded courtyard next to Molly's. The house on the lot was empty for renovations, so we would have some privacy in case I needed to kill him. In the shadows, I turned and faced him, resting a hand on my hip.

"So…you want to confess?" he asked, arching a fuzzy, black eyebrow.

I shook my head. "No, I want you to take me to them."

"Take you to who, devushka?"

"The Dominion leaders. Don't play dumb with me," I grated. "I know you know who I'm talking about."

He grinned, appearing intrigued. "Vladychestvo, huh?" A low, amused chuckle bubbled from his chest. He shoved his meaty hands into his pockets and peered down at his shiny, black shoes for a moment. "I'm afraid you'll have to be more specific, girl. We are many," he said, peeking up at me from under his brow.

I slowly slid one of my hands across my stomach, hooking my forefinger into a loop in the center of my belt buckle. When I dropped my hands to my side, I dragged the short blade I had concealed in the design of the buckle out of its sheath and hid it in my palm.

"How about the Saints—Svyatyye? You're one of the leaders, aren't you? You can, at least, get me to the leader, if you're not. You get me to the boss, and I'll confess, I'll do whatever you want." The prickle of an approaching presence drifted across my neck.

Dultsev raised his gaze and smirked, stepping closer. He was within striking distance now, but I held my position.

I needed to find the reason my mother ran, the reason I am the way I am. I needed to make sure they wouldn't go after Dean's family. If that meant cutting the snake off at the head, I would do it. I wasn't so naïve to think Dultsev was the head honcho, but I had a feeling he knew who was.

"Vhatever I vant? Really?" he asked, feigning pleasant surprise. His happy mask soon turned to a scheming expression. "Oh, devushka." He made a disappointed sucking sound through his teeth and shook his head. "You'll do anything I vant because I tell you to. Otherwise, your friend vill die."

An unsettling shiver rippled up my spine as I heard shoes scuffle on the ground behind me. Yellow teeth gleamed between Dultsev's curled lips, and his eyes darted beyond me.

I tried to turn, but found myself trapped in bulging biceps with a pungent-smelling cloth smashed over my nose and mouth. I slapped my palm against the man's thigh, feeling the blade slice into his muscle.

He grunted in my ear and jerked me backwards. I lost my footing. I snatched the blade out and pulled myself up using the arm crooked around my neck. Kicking at the man dragging me, I choked on a deep breath and grew overwhelmingly tired.

"Put dem in de trunk." The Russian's voice was just a distant murmur as a drug-induced fog swallowed me.

The last thing I saw over the edge of the dingy cloth on my face was another bruiser cradling a limp Betty across his arms. He ogled what lay beneath her torn bodice with a wide smile. She was missing a shoe and her head was craned back, hanging off his forearm. Her eyes were closed.

I managed a weak, muffled scream before my eyes rolled back in my head.

The Rivalry

I sprinted along the dimly lit street, my shoes pounding and scuffing against the stone as I hurried to the rear of the barbershop and down the steps to Molly's.

I had searched everywhere for Vivienne — everywhere I knew to look anyway — except the club. I'd even stopped the truck and jumped out, embarrassing myself, when I'd mistaken one lady strolling down a sidewalk downtown for Vivienne, and another getting into her car at a grocer's on the outskirt of Charleston.

Molly's was my last resort. Betty wasn't home when I checked there, so maybe Vivie came here looking for her.

Banging against the door, I yelled, "Frankie, ya gotta let me in, man. Open the fuckin' door, Frankie." I paused, hearing someone approach. I braced my hands on either side of the doorjamb and waited for the person shuffling closer.

163

The door creaked open and Frankie frowned at me. "Wha' do ya want?" he drawled.

I glanced over his shoulder at the empty tables. The band was packing up, looking rather sad, and the barkeep was stacking glasses behind the bar with a distracted gleam in his eyes. "Closin' up early, Frankie?" I asked, crossing my arms over my chest.

His weary gaze scanned the top of the stairs then looked behind him for a moment. "Yeah. 's not been a good night." He reached into his pocket, yanked out a kerchief, then dabbed the sheen of sweat building on his forehead.

In a low, urgent tone, I asked, "Where's Vivienne?"

He stuffed his kerchief into his back pocket with one hand while waving my question away with the other. "C'mon, kid. Git outta here with that, will ya? I ain't got time to be botherin' with no one-sided crush. I let ya in here before 'cause I thought you deserved a chance, but if Viv don't wanna talk to ya, then she made her decision. I got worse things to worry about." His eyes darted up to the lot above us nervously before pulling the door shut.

I threw my hand against the rickety boards and sneered at him. "This isn't some poor attempt to win over a girl I'm sweet on, Frankie. She is mine, and I'm pretty damn sure she feels the same about me. Now, if you'll be so kind, tell me where in the hell she is. I have a feeling she's gonna do something stupid and get herself in some deep trouble."

Frankie pressed his lips into a thin line, and his shoulders slumped. "I'm afraid yer too late, son."

I dropped my hand from the door. "What do you mean?"

164

He huffed out a disheartened breath. Frankie turned, leaving the entrance open, while he shuffled back toward the bar. "Al?" he barked. "Pour us some Shine, will ya. I don't know about the sailor, but I sure as hell could use somethin' strong right now."

I followed the owner in and nodded to the barkeep eyeing me.

"Comin' right up, gents." Al tipped an unlabeled brown bottle over two shot glasses and positioned them in front of two empty stools.

Frankie wiggled his plump body onto one of the seats then looked at me with raised eyebrows. "Ya gonna take a seat, son, or are ya waitin' for the hooch to come to you?"

I slid onto the stool and slammed back the shot, wincing as the fire burned my throat.

Frankie chuckled. "Go on and give the kid another, Al. He's gonna need it."

The bartender refilled my glass. I held it up, silently thanking him, before gulping the second shot down with a little more grace.

"Vivienne," I reminded him, setting my jigger upside down on the bar. "Where is she?"

Frankie downed his third drink. He dragged his hand over his mouth, scraping the gray stubble that had grown since the morning. "She waltzed her ass right in here, told one of the most dangerous men to ever walk through that door she wanted to talk, then left with 'im. We tried to get her attention," he looked at Al who mimicked his worried expression, "but, she wouldn't stop. I ordered Al to git me the shotgun, but, by the time I made it outside on my bum knee, they were gone."

165

"Dultsev?" I questioned, already knowing the answer. He was the only link that Vivie knew about for certain. Of course, she would go to him.

How could I have been so stupid?

How could *she* have been so stupid?

She had no idea what she was walking into. I only knew the bit my father had told me, which wasn't much—nor was it pretty. I was lucky I'd recognized the bastard from one of Dad's many photos and remembered enough about Dultsev's start in the Dominion to know he was a threat. He was initiated into one of the twelve sectors planting their roots into the States. As far as I knew, he'd clawed his way up the ranks at an early age by offing any who stood in his way. Now, I assumed he was sitting pretty at the top of one of those sectors.

"I made it to the edge of the lot when I heard some commotion next door. There was a lady screamin', a car pulling up in the neighbor's drive with the headlights off, then tires burnin' outta there so fast, I barely saw 'em as I hobbled into Glen and Bev's yard." Frankie nabbed the bottle from Al's hand, who seemed to be guarding it more than hoarding it, and filled his jigger up, again. "I came back down here, cleared the club, and I've been tryin' to figure out what to do ever since."

"You didn't think to go to the cops?" I asked, curious about his reply. Frankie seemed like a good guy, but I wouldn't put it past him to save face when it came to his establishment.

Al lifted a glass off the pile next to him and poured himself two-fingers worth of Moonshine.

Frankie glanced at the bartender, hesitating. "I can't. They'd start to investigate. Molly's has been around for a while now, and many unlucky souls have run into trouble in one way or another down here." His gaze roamed over the ceiling and walls slowly as if having a private conversation with the building, like it was an old friend, assuring it that he'd keep its secrets. "Some found their way to the bottom of their barrel willingly, others…," his words faded when he locked eyes with me. "I love Viv like a daughter, I do. But, Molly's…she's more than a business, son. She's the way I feed my wife and keep her on this shitty earth, the way I've raised a family, the only way I'll get to look back on all this one day and say, 'Fuck you. I'm hiding away with my Mol for the rest of our short, pitiful lives.' Ain't no ground-sniffin' cops gonna take that from me.'"

He shrugged. "Besides, if Dultsev found out I went to the police, I'd be dead before I left the interrogation room." Frankie leaned toward me, lowering his voice and said, "I don't know what that man is hittin' on exactly, but it ain't no good. I heard him talking about infiltratin' some of Charleston's city offices with his men, who were already working up the system, if I was listening with my good ear. Seems like he's plannin' on makin' himself at home here, and controlin' the strings to powerful government officials in this town. There's no tellin' which cops he's got in his back pocket already." Sliding off the stool, he paused, a glimmer of hope sparking in his eyes. "Viv's a smart girl. If she came in here and asked the devil to dance, she must've had a plan. If she doesn't…," he shook his head, "may God rest her soul."

Frankie pounded his fist on the bar twice, looking at Al. "C'mon, Al. It's time to go home. We can come in early tomorrow night to finish up." He walked away, mumbling, "I'll do anything I can to help her, kid. Let me know if you come up wit' somethin' that'll keep us all outta trouble."

I watched the older man wobble toward the stage and relieve the band. It was easy to understand his need for survival. He didn't have much, but what he did have, meant the world to him. And, though, he didn't likely have long left in this world, he deserved as much a chance as the rest of us to carry it out with his soulmate.

He was right; Vivie was a smart woman, and she was certainly capable of fending for herself—more than he really realized. I knew what kinds of things men like Dultsev were willing to do, though. I'll be damned if I let her fight them alone.

"Hey, Frankie? You got a telephone I can use?"

"In the office," he yelled absently while fixing a loose chair leg.

Al pointed toward a dark hall beside the bar.

I pulled Ivan's number from my pocket as I walked down the hall and into the small room at the end. I squinted at the bright lamp on the corner of a desk in the center of Frankie's office. Messy stacks of receipts and mail filled almost every inch of the surface. "Not a very good bookkeeper, I see, Frankie." I rounded the desk and sat in a worn leather chair facing the door.

Sifting through the pile of papers, I found the telephone under a yellow folder. I discarded the folder, picked up the receiver, and poked my finger in the top hole, winding the dial disc until I landed on zero.

The line dinged, and a throaty operator's voice asked, "How may I direct your call?"

"Ivan Markow in New York City, please."

"Sure, hon," she replied.

"Da," Ivan answered on the other end, then I heard the operator click off.

"Ivan, It's Vitson. Someone's taken her." I didn't say who, wanting to see if he'd offer up any clues on his own.

"Der'mo," he exclaimed. "Shit, shit, shit," he cursed again.

The static of his hand covering the receiver and a muffled voice speaking in the background filtered through the phone. I waited, trying to make out what was being said with no luck.

"Why didn't you kill her yet, Vitson?" The bite in his words was meant to intimidate me, yet I couldn't have cared less. "If you had done your job, we wouldn't have to worry about Svyatyye."

"Why would *you* have to worry about the Saints, Markow? Why didn't you tell me I would be up against another sector? Who exactly is it pulling the strings here?" I gritted.

He'd just confirmed they knew Dultsev was looking for her. They sent me into a gladiator's ring, knowing I wasn't prepared. There had to be something big going down if there were two sectors pitting against each other. Two brothers, sure, but for two families of the Dominion to be at each other's throats, there was something or someone much bigger involved.

A low, gravelly chuckle came through the line. "Last I checked, you gave up on your brothers, Vitson," he spat my name as if it soiled his Russian accent. "Dis is our business to attend to. Pay you no mind, traitor."

I growled and balled my fists, holding back the urge to beat on Frankie's desk. "You bastards made it my business when you dragged me in to kill her. Now, tell me where they might have taken her, dammit."

Someone spoke in the background, then I heard a laugh I recognized. "Laskin," I blurted. "I know he's there. Tell that asshole, if he wants me to take care of her, he needs to tell me where they are going." At this point, I'd let them think I was going to kill her if it meant getting the information I needed.

"Mr. Vitson, you don't know what you've gotten yourself into…what dat girl has dragged you into. We have little control over the men who have her, if they indeed have her. Regardless, you'd be better off forgetting about the bitch and going about your life."

I exhaled and pinched the bridge of my nose to release tension. "And my parents?"

He chuckled. "Someone has to pay the dues, traitor."

The line clicked, signaling the call's end. I slammed the phone onto the base, its sharp ding filling the room.

"What the hell am I gonna do?" I whispered to myself. I couldn't forget about Vivienne—my heart wouldn't let me—but, my parents…they wouldn't be able to defend themselves against these animals.

How do you choose between the loved ones from your past and the embodiment of your future?

Chapter Eighteen

My eyes fluttered open to pure darkness. I tried to swallow the mouthful of spit dribbling down my cheek, but struggled to move my lips around a thick bunch of cloth threaded between my teeth. I was gagged. Every time I moved my jaw, a knot of the fabric at the base of my skull pressed into me, worsening the hammer pounding my brain.

Numbness spread down the arm pinned under me. I tried to reposition, but my wrists and ankles were secured by ties like my mouth. My breathing sped up, matching the rapid beat of my heart.

I closed my eyes and focused on my surroundings. The foul odor of expended fuel filled the space, adding to my nausea and dizziness. My body jostled, bouncing inside a small container lined with scratchy felt. The steady purr of a motor rumbled below me. I bounced again, smacking my head into the hard floor of what I guessed to be a vehicle's trunk. I groaned, feeling like my head would explode soon. The muffled music resonating through the seat back behind me didn't make the throbbing any better.

Suddenly, the car jerked to a stop, and I rolled forward. A warm body stopped me from tumbling to the end of the trunk. I sucked in a sharp breath, when I heard a whimper next to me.

Mumbling through the cloth in my mouth, I said Betty's name, praying she answered — that the lump of flesh in the trunk with me was my best friend.

A shrill, garbled plea filled our tight quarters, but it was clear enough to recognize my own name being called. It *was* Betty.

I scooted closer to her, the rough carpeting abrading my hands and ankles as I slid. Her trembling body nestled into mine. The only thing we could do was comfort each other. I tugged and twisted my hands against my bindings, but they were too tight to escape. With the fear and emotion radiating off Betty, I knew she wouldn't be able to focus enough to even try to get her hands free.

The engine quieted, and the metal pop of a car door opening came from outside. The vehicle dipped a few times, then the trunk hood lifted.

I squinted into the morning sun. A large silhouette blocked some of the light from burning my eyes. Blinking, I focused on the form scowling down at me.

One of Dultsev's goons grinned around a mouthful of crooked teeth.

Quiet whimpers blew against my neck as Betty burrowed her face into me and shook her head, denying something in her mind. She was probably trying to work through the situation in her mind and settled on denial to get her through. I'd felt that way many times before, but, glaring up at the brute, I knew there was no amount of denying that would make things any better.

Besides, I had no intention of denying them.

His stubby, scarred fingers clamped around Betty's bicep and pulled. She squirmed and bleated out a stifled scream, fighting his hold on her. Hours of tears had ruined her normally perfect make-up, leaving black streaks down her cheeks and temples. Scraggly gold curls stuck to her face. Her tea-green eyes widened, begging me to help, but there was nothing I could do.

The goon gritted his teeth and jerked Betty up. He dragged her out of the trunk and dropped her onto the ground. A loud grunt escaped her chest on impact.

I couldn't see her anymore. I just saw the thickly muscled, broad framed man bracing his hands on his knees as he bent down and laughed at Betty's turmoil.

Narrowing my eyes in a soundless response of anger and fury, I made a promise to make that man one of my many victims.

He asked her a question in what I assumed was Russian. When she didn't answer, he slapped her. The crack of his hand meeting her cheek fueled my rage. He repeated the phrase, droplets of spit flying from his lips.

I wiggled in the trunk and yelled around my gag. His cold eyes darted up to me. I lifted my head and yelled a garbled, "...uck you."

His amused grin morphed into a sneer.

Yeah, I thought that'd get your attention.

The giant straightened, balling his fists at his sides, and stalked toward me. "What did you say, beetch?" he asked.

I mumbled a broken, "...ake...he...gag ou..."

His inserted a finger behind the wet fabric and tugged it out of my mouth. I worked my jaw for a moment, stretching my cheeks and lips. Tilting my chin up in defiance, I pronounced each word clearly. "I. Said. Fuck. You."

Anger flared in his blood-shot eyes and his teeth grinded. "If I vasn't under orders to keep you alive, you'd be dead."

Before I could reply, he shoved my gag back in place and clutched my arm. He yanked me over the lip of the trunk, the metal digging into my ribs. His grip tightened when my legs flopped along the bumper, and he took on my full weight. I stumbled backward, tripping over Betty as he hauled me across a large lot of pavement, my feet scraping the cement.

Betty wailed, rolling on the ground while struggling with her bindings. She watched the man separate us with terror in her eyes. A second man lifted her up and carried her in our direction.

My handler stopped then stood me upright, propping me on my restrained feet. I tore my gaze from Betty to look at the large structure looming over us. The sun's rays gleamed off the smooth, silver exterior of a massive cargo plane.

My heart skipped a beat.

If these thugs got us onto the aircraft, it was likely we'd never see Charleston again.

Goon number two stopped to our left and squinted up at the plane. He asked goon number one something in Russian. Goon number one nodded, then number two carried Betty to the back of the aircraft where he hiked up a ramp leading into the hull. They disappeared from my sight, and I was suddenly slung over goon one's shoulder. He barked an order to someone approaching in black slacks and shiny shoes — the pilot.

I bobbed against his back as he carried me up the same ramp Betty ascended. It was a dark, dirty space filled with stacked boxes and crates. Chickens squawked from somewhere I couldn't see.

My handler dumped me on the floor, plopping me down between two towers of crates tied to loops protruding from the planes interior. I winced, my rump smarting from the impact.

Betty's sobs echoed off the rounded walls as goon number two untied her wrists and refastened them to a tie-point above her head. Her red-rimmed gaze stared up at the somewhat handsome thug bending over her. If we'd seen him at the Oceanside Restaurant, she might have seduced him. In this light, though, she was shooting daggers at him with her eyes.

The thug situating me kicked my legs to the right then shoved his hands under my arms and lifted me so I was sitting ramrod straight. He pulled my fists around to one side and untied the ropes on my wrists. Raising my hands, he threaded the end of one rope through a loop two feet above my head then tied it to the other end in a sturdy knot.

I could've tried to escape while the bindings were loose, but the voice in my head urged me to comply. The feeling in my gut said they would lead me to the men who started all this. I felt sure Dultsev was just my way in.

I hadn't expected to be kidnapped, but if it got me where I intended to go in the end, it was a small change in my plans to accommodate. The problem was figuring out how to get Betty out of this alive. She would be my Achilles heel.

Goon one squatted down in front of me. I remained calm and compliant, searching his eyes while I considered the many ways I might bring him pain in the near future.

"You *are* a pretty little cunt. I can see why they fall into your trap," he confessed in his overbearing accent. He traced a finger along my jawline, his gaze dropping to my parched lips.

I smiled the best I could with the soppy cloth bridling my mouth. I refused to show how deep under my skin he'd managed to crawl. It would give the creep too much satisfaction.

My cool response discouraged his ogling. He patted my cheek with his fingers in a patronizing manner before standing up. "You be goot little girls now. Ve'll be home soon." He grinned then turned, nudging his chin at the other bastard smoothing his hands down Betty's torso, copping a feel of her breasts. "Come, Detrick. Ve've got a long ride ahead. You'll have plenty of time to play vhen ve are in de motherland."

I bit down on the rag, fighting the urge to shout at goon two. Betty cowered from his touch, burying her face in her bicep. He ignored goon one's command and moved his thumbs over her nipples in gentle circles as if they were alone and had all the time in the world.

"Detrick," my thug barked.

Detrick leaned forward and whispered something in Betty's ear, then stood. He licked his lips, seeming to commit the scene of Betty tied up and helpless to memory, then followed the lead asshole down the ramp.

Propellers sprang to life, filling the hull with a deafening whir. What little bit of light there was crept from the space as the ramp pulled closed, sealing us in darkness.

Betty's stammered cry nearly broke my heart. I'd never have a normal life. I should've stayed away from her, should've saved her from ever being exposed to this.

Slumping back against the hard, rounded surface behind me, I lulled my head back and settled in for the long trek to Russia. I forced a note from my throat, humming Betty's favorite of my songs over the roar of our plane lifting off. Moments later, I felt my stomach leap and knew we were in the sky. I silently bid my goodbye to Charleston, my father, and to Dean.

I continued humming until Betty's cries quieted.

The Confrontation

I threw back my fifth shot of whiskey, welcoming the burn flaring in my throat. Wiping the back of my hand over my mouth, I slammed the glass down and signaled for Al to pour me another.

"Dean, ya know, I usually would, but...," he glanced at Frankie who was waddling toward the door to let someone in the club, "uh, I think it's time to stop."

I pounded my fist on the bar and leaned in close to Al's face. "I don't remember asking your opinion. Pour me another, dammit."

Al didn't even flinch. He just flattened his hands on the bar and moved closer to me. "I don't think it's a good idea," he said, annunciating every word.

Thrusting the glass toward him, I growled, "Pour the fuckin' liquor, Al, before I break your face." I was well-aware the five shots and

179

two Schlitz I'd drank were slurring my words, but I didn't care. I needed to drown my sorrows. Al wouldn't take that away from me tonight.

The barkeep pursed his lips and glared at me. His fingers wrapped around the small shooter then flung it against the wall behind him. Glass shattered to the floor. "Pull it together. You've got company." His gaze flicked to a group of three men entering the club. One of them was Dultsev. "Talk to me like that again, my friend, and I'll beat the sober back into you. Understand?" He picked up a wet wine flute from behind the bar and stuffed a towel inside, drying the water from it as he watched the motley men find their seats.

Regret flooded my blurry emotions. He was right, I shouldn't have spoken to him like that. I should have kept my wits about me. Now, I wanted to pound the arrogance out of the fat Russian, but I wouldn't be able to enjoy it without a clear head.

I took a swig of my warm beer to wash down the regret and turned to face the packed club.

Dultsev hunched over his big belly, resting an elbow on his table. He appeared to be discussing business with the two men sitting with him. They nodded periodically, saying little in return as Dultsev spoke. One gent, older with white hair and a lean build, smoked a pipe clamped in his teeth. The other was much younger and resembled the smoking man.

A lady in a pink chiffon dress wandered over to their table and rested a gloved hand on the older gentleman's shoulder. "Mayor," she chimed, "I didn't expect to see you here." The woman giggled with delight. She bent down to his ear like she was going to tell him a secret, but didn't lower her voice at all when she spoke. "Don't worry, I can keep a lid on it."

Somehow, I doubted that.

The mayor gave her a nervous smile and nodded. "I'd appreciate it, Nadine."

"Who's your friend," she asked, eyeing Dultsev with curiosity.

"Oh, he's just an acquaintance," the Mayor replied, clearly trying to avoid telling the nosey woman. "See you in the office on Monday." He waved her off, turning away from her to face Dultsev.

Nadine frowned, but took the hint and moved on to another group of patrons to pester.

I concentrated on the Mayor, the cat I assumed was his son, and Dultsev. Now, why would the mayor meet with a first-rate Russian gangster? Nothing good could come of it, that's for sure. I was positive their meeting was another strategy for Dultsev to claw his way into Charleston's politics and gain power as he'd done through the Dominion families.

Broadening my shoulders, I inhaled a sobering breath and strode toward the scheming assholes. Dultsev's eyes darted up to mine and narrowed, full of triumph and contentment. A slow smile crept across his ugly face.

He thought he'd won. He thought I wouldn't find Vivienne.

One way or another, he'd tell me where she was.

I grabbed two fistfuls of his high-dollar suit and yanked his chubby ass right out of the chair. His eyes widened and a grunt left his lips when I slammed him into the wall behind him.

181

Women squealed, and chairs skidded along the floor. The Mayor and his son jumped to their feet. I glared over my shoulder. "Don't be stupid," I said. "He's not worth it."

The mayor switched his gaze between me and the Russian, considering his risks. He raised his hands in surrender, not willing to draw more attention to himself. His son clenched his hands into fists and lunged toward me, but his father latched knotty fingers around his forearm and shook his head. The young man backed off instantly but with reluctance.

The musicians silenced their instruments, realizing that their audience was mesmerized by the scene I was causing. All chatter stopped. From the corner of my eye, I noticed a few of the male patrons stand and ready themselves to intervene if necessary. From what I'd heard, quarrels broke out in Molly's all the time. They were waiting to see if we'd settle it on our own, as most did, before stepping in.

I locked my gaze on the man wrenching his hands around my wrists, trying to escape my grip. I smiled. "Where's your muscle, Dultsev?"

He stopped his useless attempts and tensed under my hold. "Dey are taking care of some business for me."

Clicking my tongue, I shook my head. "Wasn't a good idea to walk in here without protection."

Dultsev guffawed. "I'm not afraid of you."

I let go of his lapels and wrapped my hands around his meaty throat. He wheezed in a strangled breath, his eyes bulging and face reddening.

182

Women gasped. Shoes clattered on the floor as men hurried toward me.

"Don't move," Frankie shouted over the clatter. I thought he was speaking to me, but when he approached my left side, I saw his angry eyes scanning over the lynch mob preparing to take me out. "Go ahead, test me," he dared, raising a shotgun to his right shoulder. Silence filled the club. He looked at me and nodded. "Do what ya gotta do, son."

Squeezing tighter, I leaned in to whisper in Dultsev's ear. "You hear that? I'm about to strangle you with my bare hands, and there's not a damn thing you can do about it. You scared now?" I pulled back to see his response.

The Russian flapped his lips like a fish desperate for water, trying to get enough air to speak.

I squinted and tilted my head a bit. "I'm sorry. What...what was that you said?" Oh, I was enjoying this way too much.

His eyes rolled back in his head.

"Oh, no, you don't." I loosened my fingers and slapped his cheek. "I'm not done with you, yet."

Dultsev sucked in what oxygen I'd allowed and rattled out a, "Fuck you, traitor."

I tightened my grip again, appreciating the veins plumping up under his skin.

The double-barrel of Frankie's shotgun swung into sight and dug into Dultsev's temple. His eyes widened.

"Would ya look at that." I smirked. "I can loosen my hands from around your neck, but I sure can't un-pull that trigger. Care to rethink your willingness to cooperate?" My fingers relaxed a fraction.

"You won't get away with this," he rasped.

Frankie jammed the barrel harder into his head, wrinkling his skin around the tip.

The Russian grimaced.

"Where is she?" I growled, yanking him away from the wall then banging him back into it.

"I don't know," he gasped.

Frankie removed the gun from Dultsev's head, cocked it, then replaced it with his finger hovering over the trigger.

The room erupted in murmurs and gasps, again, but no one budged.

"You'll never get her. Once he has her back, he'll never let her go. You're as good as dead."

"Why don't you let me worry about that. Where is she?" I drawled.

When Dultsev noted Frankie slowly crook his finger tighter on the trigger, he sputtered, "Where it all began." I loosened my hand, and he wheezed, "Russia."

CHAPTER NINETEEN

A booming knock resonated through the cargo hold, followed by the creaking of the ramp lowering. My eyes popped open and instantly searched for Betty.

As illumination from the outside lights flooded the space, I registered movement across the floor and sighed in relief. Betty winced, flexing her slender arms to pull herself into a more upright position. She glanced at me then to the growing opening at the back of the aircraft. Her legs folded tight to her chest in a useless means to guard herself.

I groaned, pulling myself up as well. My arms had lost feeling long ago and now ached with the uncomfortable needling that comes when your circulation is compromised.

Leaning forward to see around my stiff arm, I noticed lush, white snowflakes falling against a black night. I gasped as an icy breeze drifted through the thin fabric of my blouse and sent shivers through my body.

185

Betty's whimpers began to quiver from the other side of the hull. With her dress gaping open, I could only imagine how cold she was.

The tinny sound of boots stomping up the ramp deterred my focus from my frightened best friend. The top of a gray, fur-trimmed beanie bobbled into sight. Fierce caramel eyes squinted into the dim vessel and zoned in on me.

Deep lines curving around his lips and eyes put the man in his late fifties. Curly jet-black hair accented by strands of silver framed his strongly masculine face. He hiked toward me, his shoulders wide and straight, holding the burden of authority. Every movement screamed control and supremacy.

He stopped next to my bound feet, studying me with interest for a few seconds. Betty's sniffles urged the man to glance over his shoulder with little more interest than hearing a leaf rustle in the wind. His steady and strangely warm gaze returned to me. "Poluchit' ikh otsyuda," he commanded, turning his head slightly toward the ramp.

My sights landed on the two red, triangular tips peeking out from under his high collar. The unwelcome familiarity of the star I was sure hid under his wool coat prickled up my spine.

The two goons who'd transported us and tied us up with the cargo hurried into view. "Da, ser," they replied in unison. The creep who had the hots for Betty kneeled in front of her and undid her restraints, a devilish smile on his face. The big brute who handled me yanked and unknotted my ties, glaring at me the entire time. They lifted us up and slung us across their arms, carrying us into the freezing night.

We followed the man with the beanie into a large compound of some sort. Satellite buildings branched out from the main building we entered. A chain link fence with barbed wire coiled along the top lined the perimeter of the site and reached at least fifteen feet into the sky.

Even if I were to get loose and escape these thugs, even if I could get Betty free, we'd have a hell of a time getting past the fence.

Dim yellow bulbs buzzed from the pan-like fixtures hanging on chains above us, lighting our way through a long hallway. Most of the dirty, paint-chipped doors lining the corridor were closed, but bright light spilled from one ahead of us. I focused on it, searching for a hint of where we were or what we were in for.

As we passed the opening, I stretched my neck back, tilting my head upside down so I could see inside. A muscled man in black pants and a bloodied white t-shirt grinned at me and eased the door closed. Behind him, I glimpsed another man tied to a chair. His face was swollen and caked with red stickiness. A weary groan bellowed from his mouth, but it only made the ruffian at the door smile wider before clicking the door shut.

Seconds later, the deafening cries of a man enduring excruciating pain echoed off the walls. Betty released a strained sob. I bit down on my bridle and inhaled a deep breath to keep my resolve. I was here to find out my past, to stop my future from killing me, to cease the dangerous need inside me. I was here for answers and blood. Damn if I'd let them make a weak woman of me.

"Awe," a smooth voice said behind me, "no cry. I be nicer to you." I extended my neck to see the goon carrying Betty, holding her tight and leaning in for a kiss. Betty wriggled in his grip and pulled away from his mouth, but couldn't escape.

I kicked and stiffened in goon one's arms, grunting and shouting through the cloth, to get goon two's attention.

My handler swung me to the side, slamming my head into the stone wall. I went limp, stars forming in my vision. I squeezed my eyes shut to correct the swirling spots and shook my head. The warm trickle of blood trailed down the top of my skull, but I ignored it and peered back at my best friend. Goon two had stopped his disgusting attempts to kiss Betty and was now smirking at me.

If that was what it took for him to leave her alone — my suffering a punishment — I would do it again.

My head ached and nausea riled my stomach as we turned a sharp left. Goon one nudged open a door around the corner with his shoulder and carried me to a rusted metal chair in the middle of a small room. He plopped me down on the seat. I huffed, ignoring the shiver skittering up through my bottom from the bite of cold soaking into my pants.

Goon two sat Betty in a similar chair positioned against the wall. While my thug worked on fixing my ties to the back of my chair, Betty's guy lowered to his knees in front of her. I tensed as my arms were stretched over the metal ledge behind me and fastened to one of the five spokes spaced along my back.

My stare never left the pervert untying Betty's ankle binds. He dragged each foot to the side, re-knotting the ropes around the chair legs. Once he was satisfied, he slipped his grimy hands up her inner calves and along the bends of her knees where he forced her legs to part farther.

Betty trembled under his touch. She squeezed her eyelids closed and turned her face away from him. She knew she couldn't stop him, that she couldn't escape, but it was probably the only thing she could do to get away. If she didn't watch him, she could hide in her mind.

His hands drifted under her wrinkled skirt and pushed it up toward her hips.

I jerked against my restraints, banging the chair legs on the floor.

The fire of a hard slap blazed across my cheek. Goon one grinned and struck me again. He bent at the waist, bringing his large, bulbous nose so close I could feel his exhales and smell his sour breath. "You don't like Lev touching her?" His grin disappeared, and he poked out his bottom lip in a feigned pout. "Dat's too bad, shlyukah." His mouth pulled into a slimy smile again. "Whores are meant to be touched."

I bit down on my gag and growled, narrowing my eyes, threatening goon one in my head with the numerous ways I planned on torturing him before I killed him.

Hysterical cackling tore me from my musings. I shifted my stern gaze to the left and found Lev staring at me over his shoulder with crazed eyes. He licked his lips like a hungry jackal then turned to Betty and lowered his head between her thighs.

She slammed her body into the chair, pushing back against the seat as if she could escape the jackal about to devour her. She sunk her teeth into her gag, holding back the fear I saw on her face, but a strained, shuttering whine managed to leave her anyway.

Lev buried his face in her sex, the only thing separating them was a thin dress and panties, then he inhaled like she was the very breath that kept him alive.

"Hvatit!" A thunderous voice barked from the door, making me jump in my chair. "Dat's enough, you imbeciles."

The room fell silent under his command. Goon one stood at attention, and goon two rose up from Betty's feet, spinning on his heels to stand at attention too.

The man from the hanger snarled at the two thugs man-handling us as if disgusted by their actions. He was too good to be true, though. All these bastards had an agenda, I could feel it. The ruthlessness radiated off them like the pungent fumes of gasoline, ready to combust at any minute.

His piercing gaze swept from Betty to me then skipped between the two lackeys. "I told you to tie dem up, nothing more. He doesn't vant dem harmed." The implication of *yet* hung heavy in the air.

I had no delusions that we'd be treated nicely while we were here.

"He vas only checking her bindings, Viktor," my goon stammered.

The head-honcho held up his hand, dismissing any further excuses. Goon one pressed his lips together, but his nostrils flared, indicating he did not enjoy following this man's orders.

"Get out of here," Viktor demanded with rich inflections. "He'll be here soon. You don't vant to piss him off, do you?"

The two thugs shook their heads. They stalked toward the door, looking like toddlers who just got their favorite toys taken away.

Lev glanced over his shoulder at Betty before leaving the room and slowly dragged his tongue along his upper and lower lips. It was a promise that he'd find a way to have her.

I'd kill him first.

.

CHAPTER TWENTY

"Are you hungry?" Viktor asked, measuring our appearances.

Betty sniffled but didn't nod, though I knew she was probably starving. My own stomach had growled non-stop for a few hours last night during the flight, but now I was so far past the point of hunger that I wasn't hungry anymore.

Viktor swung a leather satchel from his shoulder and stooped on one knee, digging through the contents inside. He pulled out a fist-sized object wrapped in paper and a silver thermos.

Walking toward me, he peeled back the crinkled paper and revealed a small loaf of bread. Viktor inserted a finger between my gag and my cheek, tugging it out of my mouth. He held the loaf out toward me. "It's not much, but it's better dan nothing."

I stretched my jaw, opening and closing it a few times. "Her first," I insisted, jerking my chin in Betty's direction.

His rugged features hardened as his caramel eyes studied me. He, finally, nodded once and turned, carrying the bread to Betty. The second he took the gag from her mouth and held the food up to her lips, she chomped down on it. She chewed frantically, her eyes closing from the bliss of having some form of nourishment in her body. Betty tore another mouthful from the loaf and motioned for Viktor to give me the rest while she chewed.

He unscrewed the lid from the thermos and held it out, waiting patiently as Betty finished devouring the bite of bread. Stretching her neck toward his hand, she touched her lips to the thermos's rim and opened wide. Viktor tipped the vessel up, pouring water into Betty's mouth until she started to sputter.

He returned to my side and offered the half-eaten hunk of wheat to me. I kept my eyes on his, but graciously nibbled off a piece and chewed.

With a full mouth, I asked, "Is this your way of softening us up before you torture us to death? Trying to gain our trust before you rip us to shreds?"

Viktor's shoulders bounced around a laugh. "My dear girl, you have quite an imagination. You have experience vith de art of torture, do you?"

I swallowed. "Maybe."

He rested the thermos on my bottom lip and waited for me to open my mouth. I obliged, drinking the cool, crisp liquid until it was gone.

Viktor screwed the lid back on and crumpled the paper back around the small chunk of bread left. He bent, snagging his satchel off the floor, then stuffed the loaf and thermos into the main pocket.

Looping the strap over his head to hang across his torso, Viktor strode toward Betty and replaced her gag. When he came to reposition mine, I turned my head in defiance.

He clenched his teeth and narrowed his eyes. "Don't mistake my patience and kindness as a sign dat I'm a nice man, Ms. Carson. I'm truly not. I simply don't vant you to pass out vhen he comes to reclaim you." He wrangled the cold, slobbery rag back into my mouth and patted my check. "Good girl."

I glared at his back as he exited the room and slammed the door behind him. I listened to his clunky boots move farther away.

Betty let out a loud sigh of relief. She tilted her head back and closed her eyes, a tear streaming down her temple and dampening her mussed hair. Her meek shoulders shuddered. She was giving up.

I mumbled her name around my gag. Her eyes snapped open, and she looked over at me.

With my hands tied behind me and my ankles fastened to the chair, there was little I could do. I scoped the room for anything that could be used as a weapon, but all I found were some gnarled cigarette butts scattered around the floor and a dry Vodka bottle nestled against the far wall.

We were going to have to improvise.

I pushed my back into the chair and pointed my feet into the floor until I was balancing on the chair's back legs and my tiptoes. Testing my weight and capability of moving, I used my toes to pivot toward Betty, then dropped the seat down with a humph.

She raised her eyebrows, looking half scared and half hopeful.

I repeated the routine, tipping the chair back, steering with my toes, then dropping back down. Each time, I moved only an inch or two, but it was something.

The legs screeched and banged across the floor under my seated shuffles, but sometime later, I'd succeeded in reaching Betty's left side without any of the men coming in to interfere.

"…y shoe," I garbled. "…eck …y shoe."

Bettys brow pinched in confusion. She stared at me for a second, pondering what I was trying to say, then her eyes brightened. She pointed her index finger down at my foot, and I nodded. She shifted in her seat, stretching her arms down, but couldn't reach me, of course.

I hummed a noise, telling her to stop, and shook my head. She paused, looking at me questioningly. I scooted closer, my leg now somewhat behind her then inhaled a deep breath.

This was going to hurt.

Bracing myself for a jolt of pain, I shoved off with my toes so hard, my chair flipped backward, thudding against the floor. I groaned from the sharp, bruising bite of the chair and my weight pinning my arms under me.

The tickle of fingers brushing the top of my foot let me know my plan worked. I craned my head up. Betty stretched her hand out barely touching my arch. I tilted my foot, and she shoved her fingertips

196

beneath the edge of my shoe. I tilted a bit more, urging her hand in where I needed it.

Her tired eyes widened when she found the thin, long wooden handle tucked along my in-step. She worked it out slowly and carefully. Once I saw the handle in her grasp, I let my head fall against the floor and exhaled.

Maybe, I could get her out of this after all.

The click of Betty opening the pocket knife rang in my ears like a sweet song of freedom. I lifted my head and watched her awkwardly saw the small blade through the ropes binding her wrists.

A hopeful cry erupted from her chest when the last threads severed. She leaned over and quickly cut through each of her ankle ties. Tiny droplets of blood marked her shins and hands where she nicked herself in the process.

Betty hopped up from her chair, tearing the soppy fabric from her mouth, then dropped beside me. She cut through my ties with shaky hands, only poking me with the blade once.

"Now, what?" she asked, helping me roll the chair to the side so I could free my arms.

I sat up, massaging my sore biceps and shoulders. "We get you out of here."

THE CHASE

I hunched down behind a high stack of cargo crates and waited. The balmy atmosphere had sweat dripping down my forehead and temples. I wiped my face across my rolled-up sleeve and repositioned so I could see between two crates.

Faint chattering bled into the hanger as two men entered through the enormous aircraft door. The tall, lanky gent carried a notebook and pen, jotting down notes while a tough-man raddled off inventory in my home language. He mostly listed produce and industrial goods, but, at the last minute, asked the note-taker about the precious cargo on the last shipment—if *they* had made it, and did *she* give them any problems?

I flexed my right hand, blood still caked on my swollen knuckles. Dultsev had taken quite a beating before coughing up the information I needed. When I left, Frankie had the bastard cuffed to the toilet at Molly's, nearly drowning in his own blood.

The squat fucker had spilled all the details about where Vivienne was being taken, who was running the show, and he even told me how to get there. Earlier that day, he had scheduled a flight to deliver stolen cargo to a small town on the outskirts of Moscow. Now, I was patiently waiting to procure the aircraft and the pilot.

Listening to the two baboons check the plane specs and baggage, I dismounted my Browning HP's magazine, slid bullets into it until it was full, then pushed the mag back in place, careful not to make too much noise.

The men finished their rambling a few minutes later, heading their separate ways on a joke about the thin man's girlfriend. The lanky fellow jogged out of the hanger, meeting up with a night guard passing by. The beefy pilot climbed the ramp into the plane.

I sprinted along the shadows, keeping an eye out for anyone who might come into the large building and interrupt my plans. Once I made it to the back of the aircraft, I hid under the ramp and peeked around the edge to make sure the jerk wasn't in sight.

Hearing the pilot banter with somebody on the radio in the cockpit, I gripped the ledge and hoisted myself into the cargo area. I crouched behind a box of apples topped by a wire cage with two clucking hens inside.

The pilot rattled off a systems-check and verified coordinates. "That's right, Misha, arriving in Moscow. They'll be there to pick us up?" he asked in Russian. The voice on the radio assured him of his ride.

"Great. We'll leave as soon as Peter finishes taking a shit," he chuckled. "The girls made it okay?"

"Yes. He should be in by midnight to get them," the voice resonated through the static.

My blood boiled. I ground my teeth and drew in all the self-restraint I could muster. I couldn't put a bullet in this asshole's head now — the plane was too big for me to fly on my own.

The pilot signed off the radio and flicked a few switches, preparing for flight. "Come on, Peter. Pinch it off already," he mumbled.

We couldn't wait on Peter. Two men would be a challenge to keep in line during such a long flight. I had to get to Vivienne and Betty.

Slinking into the cockpit without notice, I snuck up behind the tough-guy and dug my Hi Power into his right temple. His hand stilled, and his body stiffened.

"Close the ramp," I ordered.

Nodding, he held up his hands then slowly moved to flick a lever marked CARGO. Pops and mechanical rolling behind me indicated that the ramp was raising.

"Do as I say, and I won't shoot you. Understand?"

The pilot's jaw tensed as he thought about his answer. "I can't fly this thing by myself."

"I'm going to be your backup. Now, get this thing going." I lowered into the bucket seat next to him but kept my gun trained on his head.

From the corner of my eye, I saw his hand jut out. He pounded his fist into my forearm, trying to dislodge my gun. I yelled, but held my gun tight as my hand smacked into the control panel.

On instinct, I leapt out of my seat, and charged the man rising next to me with anger in his eyes. I swung my left fist out, connecting with his jaw. He swayed back then regained his balance and lunged for me. I ducked, narrowly missing his right hook. Thrusting my pistol hand out, I bashed the butt of my gun against his nose. Blood gushed from his nostrils. He cupped his face, groaning in pain.

Apparently, he underestimated me.

Pointing the business-end of my Browning between his eyes, I said, "Sit down, get this fucking bird in the air, and I won't give into the urge to shoot you in the face."

His gaze focused on the barrel. He toppled down into his seat, took a deep breath, and began engaging the engines. His hand reached for the radio.

"Not unless you want a finger blown off," I gritted, aiming for his bare ring finger.

"I...I need to make sure the way is clear," he stuttered.

"We'll see if it's clear when you get this tin can outside." I wasn't taking any chances.

He pulled his hand back, continuing his work with the instruments. I assisted while keeping my gun on him.

Before too long, we were rolling out onto the runway and gaining speed. The force shoved me back into the seat. The nose of the plane lifted, carrying us into the air, and my stomach fluttered.

I grinned at the blood streaked meat-head glaring at me. "Get comfortable, it's gonna be a long ride."

Chapter Twenty-one

Easing the creaky door open, I smushed my face into the crack and assessed the potential danger. The dirt and cobweb riddled hall was quiet — they didn't even post a guard outside the room. They obviously didn't know me well.

I looked over my shoulder at Betty and held out my hand to her. She locked her fingers around mine, accepting my lead. The hinges squeaked as I shouldered the door open more and pulled her through with me.

We pressed our bodies tight against the walls, creeping toward the direction I remembered the goons bringing us in from. Up ahead, there was a corner we'd have to turn. I slowed, glancing back at Betty who was gnawing on her lower lip to hold the fear I felt in her tense hand at bay.

Nodding, I tugged my hand from hers and motioned for her to stay where she was. She wrapped her arms around her stomach and gave me a look that said she would stay, but she wasn't happy about it.

I smiled, hoping it would help her feel safer in some small way. Inching toward the corner, I listened for voices and shoes clacking against the cement floor, but it was silent. Chancing the exposure, I snuck a quick look just past the edge of the chipped brick. I yanked my head back and flattened myself to the wall, staring at the ceiling.

How was I going to get us past Lev?

Bet tugged on my sleeve, worry and make-up streaking her face. I inhaled a deep breath then forced it out. Shoving Betty back to the room we came from, I thought about how I might be able to use her as bait.

Leaving the door cracked so I could still hear anyone approaching. I unbuttoned the bottom of my shirt and tied the tails in a high knot to showcase my midriff. I took the knife from my pocket and thrusted it at her. "Take this."

Her brows shot up. "What in the hell am I supposed to do with this, Viv? It's a goddamn pocket-knife."

I fisted the torn edges of her dress bodice and yanked, shredding the fabric farther. She gasped, gawking at the front of her brazier. "Vivie," she whined, "what in the world are you doing?"

Fussing with her hair, I replied, "Honey, God gave you some great assets…if ever there was a day to flaunt them, today is it." I smudged the mascara lines from under her eyes with my thumbs, then leaned back and studied her, approvingly. "I think you're presentable."

"Presentable?" she squawked. "I don't know about you, but I was taught a lady didn't walk around with her undergarments on display."

I rolled my eyes. "Cut the shit, Bet. We both know how much you love to *display* that body of yours when it's for a potential lover. Don't get all square on me now."

Snatching her wrist up, I repositioned the blade in her hand. "Hold it like this. Remember, aim for the neck, eyes, or balls." I stared at her with unblinking eyes to make sure she understood the gravity of what I was saying.

She shook her head, her face scrunching in confusion. "Wha...what are you talking about, Vivie?"

I placed my hands on her shoulders and squeezed. "Lev. He's around the corner. I need you to be the distraction. If I can't get to you in time, I want you to use this to end him," I explained, lifting her knife-wielding hand in front of her face.

Betty's bugged eyes focused on the three-and-a-half-inch blade as if it were a weapon from the future, and I'd just asked her to end an alien invasion with it. "I...I...No, Viv."

"Betty, I'm going to get you out of here, but you have to help me out a little, darlin'."

Reluctantly, she cinched her lips together and nodded, horror and uncertainty clear in her glossy gaze.

I flipped the jagged edge of her dress open completely and jutted my chin toward the door. "Let's go."

Escorting her back into the hall and to the corner, I homed in on our target. One more quick glance around the corner, confirming that no one had joined Lev, and I urged Betty forward.

She gulped down her fear, pushed up her perky breasts, and set into a sultry sway that was sure to get Lev's admiration.

Beyond the edge, I heard Lev mumble his shock to see Betty, followed by his purr of arousal.

"I was hoping to find you," she said in a saccharine, southern drawl.

"You've found me, baby. Vhat do you plan to do vit me?"

Betty's abrupt gasp and the thud of chests bumping together let me know he'd likely captured her in his arms. When I poked my head around the corner again, rage bubbled to my surface at the sight of the filthy asshole pawing all over her. She was too busy trying to keep his slobbery mouth off her to remember the knife in her hand.

I marched toward them, slipping the hairpins out of my curls. My long locks cascaded down my shoulders, bouncing with each angry step I took.

When I was within arm's reach, I yelled, "Lev!"

He jerked his head around, and his mouth opened as if to shout to his comrades. Before the first syllable crossed his lips, I pulled back my elbows and propelled them forward, flattening my hands over his eyes.

Betty wrenched free of his grip, cupping her shaking hands over her mouth to stifle a scream.

Lev stumbled back, his face frozen.

I clutched his shirt, smirking, taking pleasure in seeing the small ruby roses poking out of each eyeball. Considering the gem-embellished pins were about four inches long, I was confident that they pierced brain matter.

Leaning closer to him, I whispered in his ear, "You should've kept your filthy hands off her." I released his shirt. He slumped down the wall into a limp pile of gutless man.

"Let's get outta here, before more of them come," I urged, grabbing Betty's wrist and tugging.

We hurried around another corner and met a stunned, burly ginger with a clump of tobacco pocketed in his lower lip.

He gathered his wits, and an impish smile spread over his tar-stained teeth. Putting one clunky boot in front of the other, he stalked toward us.

I let go of Betty's hand, and rolled my shoulders back to thrust out my breasts. Matching each of his steps, I sauntered forward, eyeing the door just beyond the brute.

A crisp whistle rang into the air while his eyes scraped up and down my body. I stifled the shiver starting at the base of my spine, refusing to allow him the satisfaction of rattling my bones. I'd not give him a chance to make me feel inferior in any way.

I licked my lips and winked, my hands drifting along my collar then grazing the full crests of my breasts. His gaze followed the curves with my fingers, mesmerized by my ample bosom.

We circled each other like two lions in a stand-off. I nuzzled into his rounded belly and combed my fingers through his course, red hair.

That familiar hunger for blood sparked to life and burned a sour path to my chest.

I smiled and stretched up, hooking my arms around his neck. The stench of his breath had me swallowing bile.

A low purr rumbled against my torso, followed by a choking gasp. His dull, green eyes widened with shock and pain. His body grew rigid. His fingers dug into my back, bruising the flesh there. A sticky string of brown saliva trickled from the corner of his lips as he struggled to get words out.

He dropped out of my arms like a three-hundred-pound sack of flour.

I squatted and shoved him onto his side, snatching the pocket-knife I'd planted between his vertebrae. When I stood, he flopped back, staring at the ceiling with a peaceful, blank expression.

"Well, well, devushka. I guess our training didn't go to waste after all."

My spine went ram-rod straight, my muscles bunched at the recognition of a voice I had not heard in decades.

Years of buried childhood memories came flooding with just one sentence spoken from this devil on Earth. How had I forgotten the endless nights of bribing for sexual favors, coercing to murder, commanding me to lie, steal, and cheat anyone who opposed the Vladychestvo—all at such a naïve age, little more than a toddler.

It was as if my mother's death had jarred me so severely that I couldn't take anymore. My mind and heart were on overload, so I just turned the key and locked the betrayal, pain, and memories behind a door of deceit. Unfortunately, deceiving myself of what I truly was couldn't stop the urges, what I'd been preened to do.

I slowly pivoted on my heel. Betty stood two paces away, body quivering with distress, her gaze bouncing between me and the group of men several feet behind her — two gun-wielding bodyguards, goon one, and *him*.

My gaze panned over the four faces of my enemies, searching for weaknesses I could use to my advantage.

"Boris," I greeted in a casual tone.

The loud drumming of blood in my ears reminded me that I needed to get a handle on my crumbling emotions. I couldn't let them see the devastation lurking under my skin.

Boris looked down at the hefty man heaped at my feet and smirked. "I never really liked him anyway."

His hair was silver, now, with faint traces of the ebony it used to be. He still slicked it back, though. Deep lines crinkled the outsides of his eyes and around his mouth, eroded by a lifetime of laughter, I gathered.

You wouldn't think such a dangerous man would smile much, but, thinking back on it, I rarely remember him any other way. I guess, when you have the power to decimate armies, there's not much that stamps a man's morale. I remembered him smiling when he was angry too — it held definitively different characteristics though.

Boris lifted his foot and cautiously put it down one pace closer to me, eyeing my movements the entire time.

"Betty," I whispered.

Her focus tore from the intimidating leader of the crew and landed on me.

"RUN!" I shouted.

The men all lunged in her direction, but she'd already set into a sprint toward the door.

Chapter Twenty-Two

Boots scuffled across the floor. Betty's panting faded as she gained distance. An earsplitting percussion of guns fired, leaving behind the smell of burnt gunpowder. The seconds seemed to pass at a slug's pace, allowing me to assess everything about the chaotic scene playing around me.

Goon one and a bodyguard shoved by me on my right. I ducked and thrust my leg out, sweeping it under their feet. They barreled into each other and bounced off the wall, fumbling to a groaning pile on the concrete. The other bodyguard aimed his gun, squeezing off another shot in Betty's direction. I leaped at him, knocking him off balance. Before he could get up, I scurried up his body to straddle his legs. I pounded two good punches into his jaw, earning pained groans in return.

"Vivienne!" Betty squealed from the end of the hall.

"Get out," I ordered, glancing over my shoulder. She hesitated, her fingers wrapped around the door handle. "Run!" I pleaded.

Goon one and the first bodyguard scrambled up to their feet and darted toward her. I pushed against bodyguard two, but he latched onto my arms, thwarting my attempt to help Betty.

"Stupid, suka," Boris snarled, reaching down to clutch my bicep.

I kicked furiously at the man beneath me while twisting in Boris's grasp. Boris hoisted me up beside him.

Panting and grunting, I pried at the iron-like fingers keeping me in place. Betty flung the door open just before goon one reached for her. I held my breath, praying she'd make it over the threshold before she was caught.

She inhaled a sharp breath, stopping abruptly. My stomach knotted. She tilted her head back, body shaking with defeated cries, and looked up at Viktor.

Boris's gruff laughter chafed my ears. I glowered at him, picturing the ways I would stab him in the neck, or peel his scalp off while he was still alive, or pierce him with every knife I could find in this God-forsaken place, or maybe burn his entire body, one inch of skin at a time.

"You may have escaped me once before, but it von't happen again."

Gathering all my saliva into a puddle in my mouth, I leaned back and spat in his face.

He chuckled with a disgusted expression, wiping the spit off with his free forearm. "Classy, my dear. Classy. I guess you are as much of a vorthless, piece of trash as your mother vas."

Fury shot through my heart. I pulled against his grip, using it to anchor my weight as I swung toward him and propelled my knee between his thighs.

His fingers uncurled from my upper arm. I received an instant of satisfaction when his skin took on a green pallor. He bent forward, groaning through the pain of me attacking his balls.

"You may not have killed my mother, but she died because of you. One day soon, I will make you pay for it. I promise."

The body guard rose up to capture me. I kicked my leg out high and to the side. The sweet crunch that followed my heel connecting with his nose, and the blood gushing from his nose, coaxed a smile to tug at my mouth. He cried out, his hands flying up to cradle his face.

I set my sights on the end of the hall and raced toward Betty. The other bodyguard and goon one posed as a shield between me and her, waiting for my assault.

Behind Betty, Viktor raised his hand to her head, pressing the glinting barrel of a pistol to her temple. Her eyes widened with terror, tears pouring down her face.

I skidded to a stop, recognizing a distinct change in her expression. I'd seen it before, the moment when a victim accepts their fate. They realize their life is at an end and give in to the thought. It comes with the glossy sheen of their gaze. Their muscles relax, despite the tension of the situation.

Shaking my head, I tried to urge her to stay with me, to keep that shimmer of hope, but it was useless. I took a cautious step forward.

Viktor narrowed his eyes and dipped his head, clicking his tongue. "You're smarter than that, girl." He cocked the gun in his hand.

The smell of expensive cologne and hostile heat rolled in behind me. My shoulders slumped. We were trapped...again.

Lifting his gaze to the presence behind me, Viktor said, "Pavel spotted a plane dat landed a kilometer outside of de fences. It was one of ours but, dere was an unexpected guest on it. Ve put him in de basement."

Boris nodded, exhaling a frustrated breath. He yanked my hands behind me, securing them with handcuffs this time. Barking orders to the other men in Russian, he dragged me deeper into the building.

I stumbled along, glancing over my shoulder. Viktor directed Betty in the same direction we were traveling. Her face was emotionless, numb-looking. Her tears had stopped. She didn't fight him, just stared at her feet.

We followed the corridor to a metal staircase leading downward. I squinted into the dimly lit area, grimacing from the musty odor hanging in the room. My eyes traced the tracks of lightbulbs wired to the ceiling, half of them were burnt out or broken with sharp edges protruding from their bases like shards of ice.

It had been some time, but I remembered the basement from my childhood. In the dark corner to my right, I could almost see the ghostly image of my mom huddled there, crying for me, like she did last time I was here.

Boris led me between two thick cement columns that braced the ceiling and brought me to a spot at the back of the room.

My gaze landed on a man stretched onto his tiptoes by restraints attached to a rafter. A black cloth covered his face, yet the flex of his arms, the way his muscled chest expanded around each heavy breath, his general stance, seemed familiar to me.

The hooded man's head rested to the side as if sleeping. A new guard stepped out of the shadows, hefting a large bucket full of murky water that sloshed over the edges and pattered to the cement floor with his movements. He approached the man hanging, grabbed the bottom of the bucket, then tossed the contents onto the prisoner.

Spasming to life, the hooded man raised his head and groaned the moment the water splashed into him. It soaked through his dark slacks and white t-shirt, causing them to cling to his quivering body.

"Where is she, you bastards?" he rasped.

I froze at the sound of his voice. My eyes drifted to the thin sheet of fabric stuck to his chest and noticed the faintest hint of a red shape with six points bleeding through.

Dean.

"Stupid boy. Did you think ve didn't know you vere coming after her?" Boris handed me off to goon one then prowled around Dean in a slow circle, his face twisted in a scowl the entire time. "You are izmennik. Vhat makes you think ve haven't kept tabs on you since you left. Ve vere just vaiting for the right moment to turn your vorld upside down. You made it so easy for us. Now, you vill pay."

Dean's head flicked to the side, following Boris's voice and shoe scuffles. "You son of a bitch. Just let her go. You can have me," he pleaded.

"Funny, dat's vat your parents said for you ven ve visited dem last veek." A low rumble of a laugh built in his barreled chest until it burst out in a hysterical chortle. "Ve didn't appease dem either."

Betty didn't know who Dean's parents were, but that didn't stop a soft gasp from escaping her. I looked over at her, still held captive by Viktor's pistol, and frowned at the tears trickling down her cheek. She had such a kind heart. I wished she'd never met me. I wished she was at home right now, enjoying a night with a new beau. Instead, she'd be forever tainted by the disaster that is my life.

I dragged my focus back to Dean. His body slackened against the restraints. His head fell forward in silent grief. I wanted to go to him, to comfort and console him, but the big goon latched onto me. I fought against his grip, squirming until my arms bruised under his fingertips.

Boris turned to the bodyguard at my left and nodded once. The guard slid a knife from the sheath fastened to his belt while marching to me. He gripped my wrist, breaking it lose from the goon's hold, and slapped the knife's hilt against my palm.

"You have a choice to make, devushka."

The way he called me devushka made me want to vomit. It brought back that feeling of being young and innocent—naïve; all of which I wasn't anymore.

"I raised you, took you in and cared for you. Your cunt mother took you from us as if she had any right. She stole from de Vladychestvo. She was too much of a coward to pay her dues. But, now..."

My fingernails dug into the wooden handle as I pictured sliding the wide, jagged blade across Boris's neck.

"Now, you are back vhere you belong. You just have to prove yourself to us. Claim your place back in our vorld, devushka. Kill this traitor."

"If I don't?" I asked, staring at Dean's shuttering body.

"Den we'll take our payment from your friend here." His eyes snaked up Betty's frame, hungry and severe. "She'll do nicely entertaining our brat'ya."

Betty murmured a whimper of fear, her knees weakening before Viktor yanked her upright and hooked an arm around her waist. The plea in her glossy eyes broke my heart. I couldn't let them touch her. They would feed her to their brothers as if delivering a lamb to a wolf pack.

They would break her.

I glanced back at Dean, thankful his face was hidden. How could I look him in the eye now and consider murdering him? He was different than the men I'd killed before.

I loved him.

Goon one's boot dug into my back. I stumbled forward. I gritted my teeth, holding back the tongue-lashing I wanted to give him.

"Get to it, beech. Unless you vant me to initiate your pretty friend right now," goon one taunted.

I sneered at him over my shoulder, taking two steps toward Dean. He grinned at me then shot Betty a side glance, licking his lips like he could already taste her.

Boris stood behind Dean, watching my every move with a devious smile on his thin lips. "That's it, devushka. Take your rightful place as my daughter, earn your seat at my side."

My gaze flicked up to Boris, careful not to show my surprise, but the sudden tension hardening my muscles gave me away.

His expression relaxed to one of curiosity and wonder. "She didn't tell you?"

I rolled my shoulders back and tipped up my chin, feigning confidence and indifference when I was really crumbling inside. "I guess she didn't have a chance before she jumped off the side of a boat."

"Psh." He shook his head, dismissing the action my mother took to avoid leading him to me. "She vasn't vorth de breath it costed to keep her alive."

Boris stepped around Dean, stopping at my side. His hot breath wafted my hair, his very presence making me nauseous. "You, Vivienne...you are vorth your veight in gold. Think about the power you vill have at my side. Russia vill be ours. Ve could overthrow the government. You vill lure them all to their deaths. No man can resist you." His fingers curled around a lock of my hair and smoothed down to the end.

I snatched my head away, narrowing my eyes at him. "Don't touch me."

He chuckled and nudged his chin toward Dean. "Kill for me, devushka. It should be easy. You don't even have to bed him first."

Eyeing the man hanging from the ceiling, I thought about the time we'd spent together, the connection we'd made, the urges I had to kill

Dean and how they morphed into a desire to be with him forever. He was the only man who had shared my bed and made me less of a monster. Now, I'd have to kill him anyway, to save my best friend.

I stepped forward, my chest brushing against Dean's wet torso. He tensed, suddenly breathing faster from my nearness. My fingers grazed over his hood, tracing the ridge of his brow, the flare of his cheekbone, and the angle of his jaw. He leaned into my hand.

"I'm so sorry, my love. You shouldn't have come for me," I whispered.

Dean shook his head. "I understand. There's no freedom from these assholes. Save Betty." He lifted his chin, offering his neck to me. I stared at the pounding vein extending from behind his collarbone.

Could I spill his blood?

Could I carry that sin on my conscience?

The sudden thunder of gun-fire exploded into my quiet thoughts, ripping through my contemplation.

Chapter Twenty-three

Squeezing my eyes shut, I hunched inward and cupped my hands over my ears to shield from the rapid bangs blazing through the basement.

When I opened my eyes again, time slowed. Muffled grunts and groans mingled with the clacking echoes. Bright flashes penetrated the dark corners. The space filled with new bodies rushing in from the stairs.

"Vivienne," Dean shouted. "Vivienne!"

I spun around, searching for Betty. Spotting her, squatting behind Viktor, I exhaled a sigh of relief. Viktor was shooting his gun, but not at the men barreling down the stairs. He shot at Boris's men.

Boris reached out, snatching my upper arm in one hand while his other hand expertly aimed and fired at the invaders.

He dragged me with him behind one of the pillars. Chips of concrete propelled into the air amid puffs of dust as the intruders took turns trying to hit Boris.

I peeked around the edge and saw goon one lying on the floor, blood pouring from his temple, his gaze pinned to the ceiling. One of the guards slumped over a chair in the corner. His gun slipped from his laxed fingers and thudded to the floor, discharging one last shot into goon one's left leg. The floor was littered with bodies, including a few from the new group.

Everyone either found shelter or was dead. The firing ceased. The bright streaks of light stopped. My ears throbbed from the loud noise, but I still heard men groaning and Betty weeping.

Dean's limp form drooped from the bindings on ceiling, and my heart stopped for a moment. My throat thickened on the fear that he was likely shot in the cross-fire. I choked on a scream.

Tugging against Boris's grasp, I lunged toward Dean. Boris clamped down harder. "Stay," he commanded.

I sneered at my captor, then returned my attention back to my lover. "Dean," I whispered loudly. He didn't answer.

"Well, now. Looks like we have some business to sort," a rugged Russian voice echoed from a distance. He spoke with the throaty inflections of this country but pronounced his words clearly like he'd lived in the States for some time.

Viktor trained his gun in our direction, keeping his position in front of Betty.

A tall, slim man, maybe fifty-two, stepped under one of two bulbs that dodged the bullets. The golden glow highlighting his heavy brow and bad skin made his cunning expression seem even more mischievous. Two men gathered behind him, one carrying a shotgun and the other a machine gun, both aiming at us.

I glanced at Boris who had his shoulder pressed into the pillar, appearing unshaken by the stranger. He was clearly out-numbered now — four to two.

That meant I had six Russian gangsters to kill before Betty and I could be free.

"I have no business vith you, Laskin. I give de orders, and you follow. It's dat simple," Boris bellowed.

"That was the old way. I've chosen to take a new approach." Their shuffling feet stopped when they reached the center of the room.

I peeked around the edge, studying their casual moves. The lead man, Laskin, readjusted his black fedora to shade his confident eyes. He tucked his left hand in his pocket while tapping the barrel of a pistol against his right thigh with the other. He wasn't frazzled at all. He thought he had everything about this situation under his control.

"Vhat makes you tink you can come under my roof, shoot my men, and leave here alive?" Boris scoffed.

Laskin grinned over his shoulder at one of his henchmen. They smiled back, tightening their grips on their weapons. Laskin set into an easy stroll toward Dean. It didn't look like he was doing much else than walking, but I knew better. He was listening, assessing, and planning. He was a true predator, in it for the kill. Like I had been.

"A few weeks ago, a little birdie squawked in my ear, telling me you took a bounty out on a young woman. I wondered why, considering I was supposed to be your right-hand man, you didn't mention this to me. Then, someone whispered that you hired the fucking Saints to track her, *and*," he emphasized, "you didn't want her dead.

"So, I says to myself, 'Why would the leader of the Brotherhood want this dolly so bad, and keep her alive at that? 'Cause Boris doesn't leave anyone alive when he puts a bounty on their neck.'

"I decided to go outta my way to bring her in myself, because I knew you couldn't count on the Saints to do it for you. I figured, if I could find this missing Marina and bring her back to you, maybe you'd trust me enough to appoint me boss over the Brat'ya in the states."

Laskin paused a foot away from Dean, staring up at his covered face. He slowly shook his head, before continuing. "Imagine my surprise when I had my men snap some photos of this dolly. It's been years, but I remembered those hazel eyes and high cheekbones as clearly as my own reflection. She's the spitting image of her mama. Nice lady, she was. She always pitied how hard you and my father were on me as a boy. I can even see a little of your ugly mug in her now that she's older."

Boris breathed down my neck, grinding his teeth as he watched Laskin over my head. Laskin reached up and grabbed a handful of the black sack covering Dean, tugging it off. He blew out a sharp whistle when he saw Dean's bruised and swollen face. Blood dripped from his parted mouth. I cringed, pressing my eyes shut, too afraid to admit how critical his wounds were.

"She definitely inherited your thirst for blood, Boris." Laskin lightly patted his fingers against Dean's red-stained cheek, forcing me to open my eyes and verify that he wasn't hurting Dean further. "I really had high hopes for this one," he said, turning in our direction. "Quite a few of my men fell victim to her perils, before I decided you were nuts to think she could be captured alive and took out my own bounty on her. I thought the threat against this one's family," he thumbed at Dean's dangling body, "would drive him to finish the job. I guess I underestimated Ms. Carson. Tell me, Marina, what was it like killing my father? I know it was a long time ago, but you gotta remember your first kill."

Laskin took a step toward our pillar, and I noticed Boris's last man stretch up from behind a table tipped on its side across the room. He aimed his gun at one of Laskin's men, his eyes peering over the table-ledge intently.

"Are you deaf, Marina? Or, should I call you Vivienne? How did it feel cutting my father's throat?"

I sucked in a sharp breath, staring at the black sack in Laskin's hand.

His father was the man under the hood over three decades ago. The one I'd murdered when I was barely old enough to hold a knife. My gaze darted to Laskin's eyes. They were surrounded by creases and yellowed by liquor and age, but I saw a familiarity in them. His dry lips spread, revealing a mouthful of bad teeth as he waited for me to recall our past.

Boris's hand tightened around my wrist. "Your papa vas a dirty rat, Anton. You vere lucky I took you under my ving. It vas nothing personal. I just knew you'd be too veak to keep your emotions from ruining my plans, so I didn't involve you in my hunt for Marina. But you had to stick your nose in business dat wasn't yours, didn't you?"

I squinted at Laskin, reversing the effects of time in my mind. I sucked in a gasp when I realized he was the young man who delivered me to a room full of men that devoured my innocence. He took me to the bastards who toyed with my privates and taught me what sex was about before I could even feel an ounce of arousal. He was the asshole who knew I'd be ruined by the terrible ways those bastards violated my mind and my body. My stomach cramped around years of sour disgust and misery. He, under Boris's orders, carried me into a world that etched the craving to kill anyone who sought me sexually into my very soul.

"Not my business?" Laskin yelled before looking at his men and laughing. "Not my fucking business, he says."

His menacing tone sent a shiver snaking up my spine.

Laskin rushed forward, lifting his pistol in my direction and cocking it. "She ruined my life. You took from me, Boris. You stole my father, you ripped my innocence from me, you ended any chance of me growing up as a respectable man. I thought, if I just did what you said and followed your lead, I could destroy you from the inside." He chuckled humorlessly. "But you just kept getting more powerful, harder to undermine. I've waited decades to stomp on you like the pathetic piece of shit you are." Laskin's eyes slid up my body with a hatred that prickled my skin. His lips pulled back from his teeth in anger. "I wanted to know for sure that whatever I did to avenge my father would crumple you to the core. Now, I will take what's yours for good."

Kapow. Kapow.

I curled into myself, clamping my hands over my ears as fires blasted through the room again. Chunks of brick exploded from the pillar, pelting my head and arms. Boris slung me to the ground, aiming his own gun at the shooters.

Betty's screech called my attention to her. From around my elbow, I saw that she was hunched against the wall, curled into herself as I was. Viktor shot at Boris's man behind the table, sending splintered wood flying into the air, but missing him before he ducked down.

Boris's thug raised his hand just over the ledge of the table and shot once, twice, without looking. The jerk with the machine gun toppled in the center of the room. Blood gushed from a hole above his left eye, pouring to the floor like a spring.

A loud clack, clack rang in my ears. I jerked with each shot from Boris's handgun. He spewed a slur of curses at Laskin who was returning fire from behind the pillar feet away.

I glanced back at Viktor. He disengaged the empty magazine in his gun and jammed another into the butt of his pistol then moved toward the center of the room, where most of the bullets were flying. He ducked then rolled into a summersault under the path of blasts, somehow dodging any damage from Boris and Laskin's war. When he straightened from his tumble, his sights were fixed on the man behind the table. Shooting bullet after bullet with a relentless focus, he drilled a hole into the center of the wooden slab. Boris's man sprung up, convulsing from the repetitive hits he took to the gut. Sputtering blood from his mouth, he slumped backward and landed on the floor without another protest.

Viktor dropped his weapon to his side. He whirled around, eyeing the two men hiding behind chipped and crumbled pillars. Laskin's gunfire ceased first. Boris's followed after getting in one more shot. The slide of metal against metal, then the click of them replacing their magazines and engaging bullets into their chambers overshadowed the muffled buzzing in my ears.

"Come on, Laskin. Dis is pointless. You kill my men, I kill yours. Let us sit and talk like business men. Dat is vhat ve are, afterall. Surely, ve can vork some'ting out. You vant me to give you a higher ranking? Ok, no problem." Boris eased his head around the corner to spy on Laskin's movement, turning his back to me.

He should've known better.

Viktor stalked toward Laskin, keeping his eye in Boris's direction. Laskin's other man with the shotgun slid two more rounds into the long barrel of his gun then snapped the hinge closed and aimed it at Boris.

Laskin stepped out into plain sight, careful to stay behind his shotgun man, guffawing at Boris's proposal. "There's only one higher rank left, and to get it, I have to kill you. Them's the rules, Boris. You should remember, since it was how you wiggled your scumbag ass onto that pretty throne of yours."

He raised his right hand and rested it on his gunman's shoulder, training his pistol on Boris's side of the pillar. At the same time, Viktor lifted his armed hand.

Bang, bang, bang, bang.

Chapter Twenty-four

Raising my shoulders up around my ears, I tried to drown out the loud noise of Viktor's shots. I pressed my back to the broken brick until it was over. Boris's thunderous belly-laugh broke into the smoky air to my left. He strolled out into the open, seeming to forget about me.

"Viktor, Viktor, Viktor," he said, amused. "You had me vorried. I thought you betrayed me for this vorthless sack of shit. I should have known you vould never do dat. You know vhat the true meaning of loyalty is." He rested meaty fists on his hips and strolled to the spot where Laskin lay pinned under his gunman's body. Both bled from various holes in their skulls and chests. Neither moved again.

Boris towered over the dog-pile and chuckled some more. "Vhat a vaste of man. Dat's the problem with dese kids today, Viktor, dey just can't get over stuff. Got to lay around crying about everything. Vhen ve vere young, dere vas none of dis pouting over spilt milk like little ninny babies." He kicked at Laskin's arm with his toe, scraping his pistol along the floor before it loosened from Anton's fingers.

This was it. This was my chance to take him out, to kill the man who'd turned me into the monster I am. All I'd have to do is run up behind him and catch him by surprise.

I fingered the metal buckle on my belt. Tugging the leather off the brass prong, I slid the long strap from the loops on my pants. Quietly, I threaded the end of the belt back through the buckle until it made a wide loop. I looked at Betty, mouth pressing into bloody knees that she'd tucked into her chest. Her eyes darted to mine then to the belt clutched in my hand. She nodded in such a slight motion, I barely registered it. I believed she was telling me to do whatever I had to, that she would not judge me.

Assessing the mess of men in the middle of the floor, I inhaled deeply. I'd just have to worry about Viktor. The other dumb-asses made it so easy for me. So much killing and ruin. Bodies scattered all over the dank basement.

I wasn't any different from them, though. I've killed for less than revenge.

My muscles bunched, and I sprinted toward Boris. I jumped into the air, lassoing his neck with the belt in my hand. As my knees gripped tight around his waist, I shoved him forward with my weight and yanked the belt tight.

Boris fell to his hands and knees with a strangled grunt. He swayed from left to right on all fours, trying to throw me like a bull in a rodeo. I squeezed my legs tighter around him, pulling back on the only rein I had. It was the only one I needed. The expulsion of breath and gurgling noises coming from Boris's reddening face solidified the power I had over him.

My breaths grew heavy. The euphoric sensation that rushed through my veins during a kill was close to its peak. I clenched my jaw and tugged at the strap one last time. Boris's skin purpled from the neck up, and he plopped to the ground like a bag of sand.

I closed my eyes, leaning back on my victim's rear, and exhaled a lungful of air. I was relieved...exhausted...elated. When I opened my eyes, I realized that Viktor was standing where I saw him last, watching me with indifference. Betty had snatched up Laskin's gun and pointed it at Viktor, but he didn't seem to care.

"Betty, give me the gun, dear," I said in a calm, breathy tone. I didn't want her to take a life. I didn't want her to carry that burden. My conscience was already tarnished; what would one more man dead by my hand do?

"I've got it, Vivie." Her voice trembled as much as her hand, but she kept her focus sharp on the only thug left in the basement.

"No need, Miss Betty. I'll not hurt you two anymore." Viktor held out his hands in surrender and slowly bent to place his weapon on the floor. He took three long, easy strides away from the gun, hands still in the air.

"I can't possibly let you go. This has to end. You'll just tell the others, and they'll come after us. I will not have her running for the rest of her life. You must understand that." I pushed off Boris's corpse. Side-stepping toward Betty, I studied Viktor.

A smile played at his lips. His relaxed demeanor and cavalier attitude almost made me angry. "Do vhat you must, but I vill not harm either of you if you do not vish it."

I quirked an eyebrow, eyeing him doubtfully.

"Regardless of vhat I did before, my only intention vas to keep you safe. I've had enough of dese dictators controlling our bratstvo like ve are dogs. Dis vas not vhat ve came together to do years ago. Ve are supposed to serve each other — protect each other. I believe you can help us get back to dat." When I didn't respond to his crazy talk, he continued. "I vill serve you from now on. You vant to kill me? Go 'head, I'll not stop you. But, I can give you all de information about the inner vorkings of dese gangs better dan anyone. You could clean out de beetches dat keep pissing on our names and taking for demselves." He spat on Boris's body, glaring at him with a deep revulsion. His eyes softened when he looked up at me again. "I vas dere de night he turned you into a killer. I vas dere vhen he tore your mother's vorld apart. She cried in my arms for hours. Ve vere good friends, your mama and I." Viktor smiled fondly at the thought.

I mulled over his words, biting the inside of my cheek to keep my mouth from gaping open. Memories of a much younger, more powerfully built, Viktor flashed through my mind. In the shadows, a man held my mother as Boris ordered me to kill Laskin's father, then Anton carted me off to meet the horde of men that would do unspeakable things to the child I was. When I had glanced back at my mother, I could see the shade of a frown on the man restraining her. A glimmer of remorse in his eyes. What I thought was someone man-

236

handling her, I could see, now, was someone comforting her and keeping her from jumping into a fight she couldn't possibly win.

"So, you want me to take over your gang and weed out some of the most dangerous men in the world?" I paused, glancing down at the corpses strewn across the floor then back at him. "You do understand that I'm just as dangerous, right?"

"I do. And, it's not dat I vant you to assume de position, you already have. After he raped your mama and turned her into his weapon den made her stand by and watch as he did de same to you, dere's not anybody who deserves de power more. You are Boris's daughter, and you have killed de leader to de Bratstvo. De brotherhood is yours by right and action. Most vould have accepted you just because of your lineage, but, since you offed the leader, your seat is irrefutable."

"Most?" I questioned, narrowing my eyes at him.

He nodded, pressing his lips into a thin line. "Dose of us who follow de code vill fall under your orders vithout protest. De beetches dat created deir own code to undermine vhat ve stand for, dey vill be harder to convince. No matter dough, I vill help you convince dem." Viktor slammed his right fist into his left palm as if to punch someone in the face.

"So, what, you want to be my right-hand man?"

"No," he proclaimed, "I vant to be your back. I vant to be de crutch upon vitch you carry your burdens and find your strength. I can show you how to become de veapon you vere meant to be, vithout the veakness of uncontrollable impulse."

A faint groan broke the silence as I considered his offer. My head swiveled to the left, and my heart nearly stopped. The sound of Dean's voice was the sweetest I'd ever heard. His head rolled up and rested against his bicep. "Viv," was all he could manage to wheeze.

"Help me get him out of here?" I asked Viktor.

He grinned, then folded an arm across his middle and bowed. "Of course. Any'ting for you, my dear."

Watching Viktor jog across the room to unfasten Dean's restraints, I placed my fingers on Betty's tremoring hand and urged her to lower the gun.

Though I wanted to shoot him where he stood for keeping Betty and I captive, it was hard to miss the pure sincerity in his tone. Everything in my gut was telling me that he meant what he said, and he hadn't done anything that actually hurt us. He may not have let us run, but I had a feeling he had his own agenda of how this day's events would play out in the end. I only hoped believing him would not put us in a situation I couldn't get us out of.

My mother trusted him, and I would have to trust her.

EPILOGUE

"Do you think they'll be okay?" I asked Dean, sliding my damp hands over my black dress pants.

He patted my knee and smiled from the other end of the backseat. "They'll be fine. Keep your mind focused on this, not what Betty and my parents are doing in Vegas. I'm sure they're having the time of their lives. Viktor put several men on them, just in case."

I nodded and inhaled a deep breath, returning my attention to the window next to me. "I know," I said, fiddling with the buttons on my cuffs. "I'm still…not used to this, I guess."

"You'll do fine. Don't give him an inch. Stay your ground, and take no guff. These men are ruthless, but you are a queen."

As the car rocked us back and forth through downtown Charleston, I straightened the crisp, white button-up shirt I tucked into my pants and adjusted the fedora I'd donned before leaving the airport we'd flown into an hour earlier.

My life would never be the same. Some of it would be worse since I'd have to constantly look over my shoulder and worry about enemies protesting my plans. Some of it would be better, though; I'd gained a sense of belonging I valued and a husband who would support me until death.

Over the last few months, Dean and I had stayed low while he healed from extensive injuries. We made love every day and married as soon as he could stand next to me at an altar.

Viktor spread the news that there was a new leader for the Vladychestvo, and that I'd be the dame taking the reins. During our recuperation time, he helped me hone my skills and self-control. I was more dangerous now than ever, but only when I wanted to be.

We sent Betty back to the states, moving her in with Dean's folks. Thankfully, Boris had been bluffing when he mentioned visiting them the night I assumed power, and Anton's men hadn't followed through with his plan to kill them before we declared them under sanctuary.

Betty didn't have anyone to keep her in Charleston, and I didn't want her to be alone. Dean said his parents welcomed the company with open arms, and rambled about how they loved having a daughter to dote on whenever he called to check on them. I'd see Betty soon enough, but now I needed to take care of some business.

"Ve are here, volk," Viktor announced from the driver's seat, scanning the dimly lit street in front of Barry's Barber Shop.

I grinned at the side of his head, feeling a sense of warmth and respect every time he addressed me by his endearment for me. After one of our most intense training sessions, he dubbed me the Volk — the Wolf — telling me that, when he looked in my eyes and felt the power behind my will, he glimpsed the wolf, the alpha, he saw in me as a child. "I always knew you'd inherit your mother's determination, beauty, and heart, but paired vith Boris's dominance and grit, you are a fierce animal," he said.

Dean popped open his door, climbed out, then closed it. Moments later, my door opened, and he reached in a hand to help me out. I rested one onyx and ivory high heel on the glistening pavement and raised myself out of the car and into the night. Viktor slammed his door beside me, heading across the road toward the cut-through next to Barry's.

I followed the two men, my heels clacking against the damp road as I stalked toward an uncertain outcome.

We'd tracked down one of his men early in the week to make certain he'd be here tonight. He was one of the last major players in the states not quite abiding by the Dominion's rules. I needed to determine whether to end his participation in our gang or to allow him to retain some small part within the Bratstvo. He could be a thorn in my side, yes, but he could also be a useful ally with so many of his political connections.

Viktor pounded on Molly's door and glanced over his shoulder at me, nodding once.

Dean squeezed my hand while I repositioned the thin blade fixed to the inside of my belt. I winked up at his gleaming gray eyes, then

241

tipped the brim of my hat low over my brow and broadened my shoulders.

The door opened. Frankie took one look at me, and his eyes lit up with pride and what I'm sure was excitement to see me alive. I'd contacted him days earlier to let him in on the plan, urging him to keep our arrival quiet. This was my first time seeing him in months, since Bet and I were kidnapped, so it was difficult for me to hide my excitement as well, but I maintained my stern façade.

He shoved back against the wall, letting Viktor and Dean slide by. I puckered my lips and blew a sweet, subtle kiss in his direction when I passed, then hardened myself for the meeting ahead.

The sultry sound of Penny's voice blending Southern melodies with smoke swirls in air immediately reminded me that this was *my* territory.

Glasses clanking at the bar drew my gaze to Al. With a firm expression, he darted his eyes to the group of noise-makers at the far corner table. Viktor and Dean both took seats at the bar and shared a drink as if they were there to enjoy the atmosphere like any other patron. They watched me veer away from them, sauntering to my target.

The crowd was dense tonight, but it made no difference to me. I knew most of these customers, and it only added to the feeling of being home. I considered this little dive my origin, the place where I found family and set into the path I was on now.

My father, James, would always be my family. He was the man who raised me and accepted my mother with an open heart. But, I didn't want him to know anything about this side of me. I enjoyed the thought of visiting him at the new cabin in the mountains I'd bought him — the farm was becoming too much of a burden, and not as safe since my new endeavors began. It pleased me to know we'd settle into our old routine of sipping tea in the mornings while reading the paper and spending our days talking as if we were two old friends who hadn't seen each other in a while, like we've always done on vacations.

This was how it would be from now on, just as it had been in my past — living two lives at one time. But, today, I had the truth of knowing I'd have support, self-control, and power by my side when it got too unbearable.

I was a goddamn tigress, after all.

"Did you hear about Georgie? They took him in on account of beating a copper and pissing on him. Got caught last night at his gal's house. We'll have to keep an eye on the inside, make sure he don't talk or nothin'," one of the greasy, bug-eyed locals informed Dultsev from across the table.

Dultsev nodded his fat head and opened his mouth to respond.

I interrupted his conversation, snatching the chair out from under a lackey sitting next to him.

The weasel-thin man fell to the floor, smacking his head on the table behind him. "What the...," he groaned, rubbing at the knot forming on his scalp.

The fellows surrounding Dultsev stiffened, taking defensive stances as they awaited orders to retaliate.

I ignored them and grabbed the back of the now empty seat, swinging it around at an angle to face Dultsev. His eyes never left mine. I lowered into the chair, leaning back like I didn't have a care in the world. Crossing my long legs, I lifted the half-empty tumbler of bourbon next to me and gulped it down.

My eyes scanned over each and every filthy, low-level gang-member circled around us. "Boys...I need a minute."

The crew of three, minus the scum scraping himself off the floor, gaped at Dultsev. He dipped his chin giving them permission to leave poor little ol' me with the Russian.

Once his men were out of ear-shot, I glanced back to see Dean and Viktor leaning their backs to the bar, palming pistols tucked in their belts.

"You are alive. Quite a feat for a woman." Dultsev rested back in his chair and sipped the gold concoction in his glass, inspecting me with curious, squinted eyes.

I slipped a thumb behind the edge of my belt, letting my hand relax there. "Oh, Mr. Dultsev, I'm more than alive. I'm living," I purred with a smirk.

He snorted. "What's this about, woman?"

"I want your respect. I want your men." Running my tongue along my teeth, I arched a confident eyebrow. "I want your servitude."

His gaze flicked up to the bar. His nostrils flared when he recognized the muscle I'd brought with me. It wasn't Dean and Viktor he needed to worry about; I was deadly enough on my own.

Tonight, he'd either surrender to me, or I'd finish his thieving, manipulating world all together.

Al showed up with a shot of whiskey and placed it on the table next to me. "From the gents over there, Vivie," he said nudging his chin toward a group of five Demony from the Brotherhood.

I had met with them in Russia to discuss my claim to Boris's throne, in which they conceded gratefully and willingly. It was a surprise to see them here, but I was thankful for the back-up. Viktor had likely made arrangements when I was otherwise occupied.

They nodded, each of them touching a finger to the brim of their hat, then continued in their banter.

Dultsev's mouth pulled into a sneer. "I'm listening," he grated reluctantly.

And that was it. I knew I had his full attention. He understood the gravity of the situation in that one delivery of a drink.

It said I had my own henchmen.

It said I had authority.

It said I was changing the way his game was played.

It said I was the fucking queen of his universe.

THE END

About Haven Cage

 Haven Cage lives in the Carolinas with her husband and son. After many years of dabbling with drawing, painting, and working night shift in the medical field, she decided to try her hand at writing.

Unfortunately, her love for books came later in life and proved to add a healthy challenge during her writing journey. Determined to hone her craft, though, she soaks up as much information as she can, spends her free time tapping away in her favorite local coffee shop, and keeps a good book in hand whenever possible.

What began as a hobby has grown into a way of escape and the yearning to take her journey farther, her love for writing and reading deepening along the way.

Haven loves to socialize and hear from her fans. Connect with her at the following links:

Facebook.com/HavenCage/

Twitter: @HavenCage

Instagram: @Haven Cage

Pinterest: Haven Cage

Look for Haven on Goodreads.com, and add her to your bookshelf!

Visit her site at www.authorhavencage.com, and sign up for her newsletter to get updates sooner, receive exclusive promotional deals, and play Haven's Puzzler for chances to win book prizes!

If you enjoyed this book, please leave a review as it is how authors succeed in the publishing world. Without the reader's love, we would be nowhere.

Thanks for your interest and support!

Books by Haven Cage

The Perilously Pretty Series

Penniless and jaded governess, Synthia James, is trapped with her employer, a man she once loved but now despises. When he bids their young housemaid to kill a man who threatens his business, Synthia's maternal instincts take over, and she commits the heinous deed herself. Now he wants her to kill again, but can she kill the man who has reawakened her long-forgotten desires?

The Faltering Souls Series

Nevaeh Richards thinks she has found a chance to leave her homeless life behind. When the spirit of the only father she knows is wrongfully taken to Hell, Nevaeh is hurled into a world haunted by monstrous demons, rogue Guardian angels, love that is beyond her control, and a soul-threatening choice between the inherent evil inside her and the faltering faith she is struggling to grasp.

Nevaeh has to face the overpowering gravity of her choice to save those she loves while striving for strength to fight her greatest threat — herself.

Trial after trial, Nevaeh's loved ones have struggled to save her from a dark destiny. The time has finally come for her to return home and join the Earth-bound angels in a war threatening to destroy the Human race. Is it really Nev who's walking the Earthly plane, though?

Made in the USA
Columbia, SC
27 June 2024

37677869R00155